Penguin Books
I Like It Here

Kingsley Amis, who was born in South London in 1922, was educated at the City of London School and St John's College, Oxford. At one time he was a university lecturer, a keen reader of science fiction and a jazz enthusiast. His novels include *Lucky Jim* (1954), *Take A Girl Like You* (1960), *The Anti-Death League* (1966), *Ending Up* (1974), *The Alteration* (1976, winner of the John W. Campbell Memorial Award), *Jake's Thing* (1978), *Russian Hide-and-Seek* (1980) and *Stanley and the Women* (1984), *The Old Devils*, which won the Booker Prize for 1986, and *Difficulties with Girls* (1988). Among his other publications are *New Maps of Hell*, a survey of science fiction (1960), *The James Bond Dossier* (1965), *Colonel Sun*, a James Bond adventure (1968, under the pseudonym of Robert Markham) *Rudyard Kipling and his World* (1975) and *The Golden Age of Science Fiction* (1981). He published his *Collected Poems* in 1979 and his *Collected Short Stories* in 1980. He has written ephemerally on politics, education, language, films, television and drink. Kingsley Amis was awarded the C.B.E. in 1981.

BY THE SAME AUTHOR

Fiction

Lucky Jim
That Uncertain Feeling
Take a Girl Like You
One Fat Englishman
The Anti-Death League
I Want It Now
The Green Man
Girl, 20
The Riverside Villas Murder
Ending Up
The Alteration
Jake's Thing
Russian Hide-and-Seek
Stanley and the Women
The Golden Age of Science Fiction (editor)
Collected Short Stories
The Old Devils
Difficulties with Girls

Verse

A Case of Samples
A Look Round the Estate
Collected Poems 1944–79
The New Oxford Book of Light Verse (editor)
The Faber Popular Reciter (editor)

Non-fiction

New Maps of Hell: A Survey of Science Fiction
The James Bond Dossier
What Became of Jane Austen? and other questions
On Drink
Rudyard Kipling and His World
Harold's Years (editor)
Every Day Drinking
How's Your Glass

With Robert Conquest

Spectrum I, II, III, IV, V (editor)
The Egyptologists

Kingsley Amis

I Like It Here

Penguin Books

PENGUIN BOOKS

Published by the Penguin Group
27 Wrights Lane, London W8 5TZ, England
Viking Penguin Inc., 40 West 23rd Street, New York, New York 10010, USA
Penguin Books Australia Ltd, Ringwood, Victoria, Australia
Penguin Books Canada Ltd, 2801 John Street, Markham, Ontario, Canada L3R 1B4
Penguin Books (NZ) Ltd, 182–190 Wairau Road, Auckland 10, New Zealand

Penguin Books Ltd, Registered Offices: Harmondsworth, Middlesex, England

First published by Victor Gollancz 1958
Published in Penguin Books 1968
10 9 8 7 6 5 4 3

Made and printed in Great Britain by
Hazell Watson & Viney Limited
Member of BPCC plc
Aylesbury, Bucks, England
Set in Linotype Pilgrim

To Philip, Martin and Sally

1

The Deportation Order arrived one clear, bright morning early in April.

'Owen?' the telegraph boy asked. 'Garret Owen?'

'More or less,' Garnet Bowen told him, feeling the bulk of the envelope fearfully. It could mean the first step on the road towards a sum of money. On the other hand it could be some newly-devised kind of recall to the colours. 'Thank you.'

Bowen, whose large and well-made frame blended with an air of inefficiency, started reading. Without preamble he was informed that the idea was excellent and he was to go ahead. He had to read to the end and scratch his thinly-haired head a lot before he saw just where excellence was being imputed. Last month, drinking with the representative of an opulent American magazine, he had helped the talk along by describing the new kind of travel article he had pretended to think desirable. And now some misinformed, progressive and well-intentioned fathead in New York had taken him up on it. He winced when he saw the size of the fee offered. Well, that finished it. He would have to go now.

Trying to smile, he hurried into the kitchen where his wife, a pretty little dark woman with strong hands and big wondering eyes, was putting a protesting child into its coat to the accompaniment of a song being sung very loudly and badly by Frank Sinatra. The noise was coming through an extension loudspeaker on the wall.

'There's some more money we can have,' Bowen bawled.

'Sorry, can't hear with this row. Oh, do stand still, Sandra.'

Bowen went back to the front of the house, no very great distance, and turned off the gramophone. 'You came, you saw, you conquered me,' Sinatra sang. 'When you did that to me I knew somehow th—' You tell us how, a part of Bowen's mind recommended. Another part was reflecting that to cut Sinatra off in mid-phoneme was not such up-roarious fun as it was with the men who did the religion at five to ten on the wireless, but it was nice all the same. It was only a pity that Sinatra could never know.

In the kitchen once more, Bowen read the telegram aloud. As he did so he began quailing internally. It had all started when, mellowed by the acceptance of a B.B.C. script and the small consequent celebration, he had let his wife reveal how much she wanted to go abroad that summer and how much good it would do them all according to her. Her mother would put up a good whack of the money, which could be recouped out of articles inspired by first-hand acquaintance with foreign matters. And getting right away from London would give him the chance to write that play. Until a couple of years ago Bowen had been supposed to be a novelist who was keeping himself and his family going on the proceeds of journalism, wireless talks and a bit of lecturing. In the last six months or so he had started being supposed to be a dramatist who was keeping himself and his family going by the same means. He had never really supposed himself to be much more than a journalist, wireless talker and occasional lecturer. But his wife disagreed.

'Well, that's fine,' Bowen now informed her at the end of his recital. 'We can do it easily now, especially if we don't take the car.' There was something fearful about having a car abroad. It would make things happen in more abundance and more quickly.

'Oh, I think we should now Mummy's offered it, and it'll be so useful with the children. We can just come and go as we please. I wish you'd take some lessons, though, and get your licence. It'd be such a help if you could relieve me on long trips. Won't you?'

'Well, I'd rather not, dear, if you could possibly manage on your own.' He had had enough experience at the wheel during his Army service to fill him with ever-renewed surprise that vehicles usually overtook one another without colliding with anything, and a little incident on the Nijmegen road one night in 1945, involving his own jeep and an unlighted lorry, could still make him whimper to himself. 'I'll give a hand with the children, take them off your shoulders a bit.'

'Mind you do, now. Well, where shall we go? Somewhere hot?'

'Yes, somewhere hot. And where there's a lot of wine. What do you think? France?'

'Well, not those mountains we went to that time. What were they exactly?'

'The Vosges. No, not there. By the sea somewhere.'

'Yes, but it's got to be really hot. Does it get hot in France?'

'In the South it does.' The word *Antibes* flared across the dark vault of his mind, quickly followed by another, shorter word. 'But it's very expensive there, you know. All the rich people go.'

'Yes, I know. Well, what do you suggest?'

'There's Spain, of course. But then there's all that filthy bullfighting to cope with. I don't really fancy that, I must say.'

'We needn't go to it, need we?' she asked him. 'Anyway, is it cheap? That's the main thing.'

'I think it is. But a lot of awful craps go to Spain. And all the Spaniards are supposed to be proud all the time.'

'What about Italy?'

'All those rotten old churches and museums and art galleries.'

'There's no need to decide now, we'll think of a place. Look, I must take this creature out before she gets intolerable. Are you going in?'

'Yes, I'm having lunch with Bennie Hyman.'

'Oh? Good job I asked you.'

'I thought I told you last night.'

'Well, you didn't. And for goodness' sake, Garnet, call in and pick up those shoes. The heels on the pair you've got on are right down. They'll be beyond repair if you keep on wearing them in that state.'

'All right, darling. See you about tea-time.' Bowen went up and pinched the ear of his daughter, who growled at him. 'Same to you, chum. You wait till you get abroad, that'll teach you.'

'It will be lovely, won't it?' his wife said, brightening up again. 'All that sun. And you getting some real work done.'

'Lovely, yes.'

At the moment, this expressed Bowen's feelings. Being pushed more or less willy-nilly out of the country in this way had, rightly considered, its points. He had a go at rightly considering these when, half an hour later, he left their South Kensington garden flat and made his way towards the centre of things. Under his arm were three books destined for return to the library. They were the translated work of three French nationals on whom, without knowing quite how this circumstance had arisen, he had recently been lecturing. Cosmopolitanism lay on every hand that morning.

'Malraux,' he had been saying the other week to his night class, 'as opposed to Montherlant.'

They had looked at him with the glum mistrust they normally reserved for his occasional announcements that, having outlined one possible approach to a subject, he was now going to indicate another, quite different from the first. The curious visiting Egyptian had glanced round at his neighbours and grinned, hunching his shoulders. At the same moment Bowen had realized that the tall dark man at the back, whom he had always taken to be a refrigerator electrician called Noakes, might instead be the French *assistant* from one of the London University colleges who was conjectured to be attending some parts of that terrible little Modern European Literature course. This realization had embarrassed Bowen and made him feel thirsty.

'Sorry,' he had said forcefully. 'Mowl-roe and Montalong.' After glaring for a time he had spelt the names out to them. Some of them had copied them down, letter by letter and glancing continually at one another's notebooks, like air-crews at a vital briefing. The curious visiting Egyptian and the tall dark man had not done this; they had written down nothing at all.

Bowen now reflected, as he got on to a bus, that trying to pronounce even a few syllables of French set off in the inexpert a most complex and deep-seated network of defensive responses. It did in him, anyway. He had a couple of days ago read a travel supplement in some weekly or other which explained that the French, although charming and so on, didn't like hearing their language spoken incorrectly or with a bad accent. (There was something similar wrong with all other nationalities too according to the supplement, which was perhaps the work of some syndicate of

British tourist associations.) Bowen made up his mind with real regret that France was out. How he wished he had shown more foresight at school. Why, at his little school, had he not spent the periods set aside for the B.B.C. Schools programmes in learning how to say the French nasal sounds instead of how to make paper aeroplanes (which in any case he had long forgotten how to do)? Why, at his big school, had he neglected *L'Attaque du Moulin* and *Les Oberlé* in favour of hiding behind the cupboard or making a book on how many times Mr Pritchard would say 'of course' and 'and so on' in the space of an hour? Education, Bowen decided, ought to be a putting-in, not a drawing-out.

While he paid his fines at the library he thought briefly about his play. There was a whole act of it, all done out in proper red and black typing, lying under his notes on Ivy Compton-Burnett in his green filing cabinet (a birthday present from his wife). He had not looked at this dramatic fragment for several months, supposedly in order to 'come fresh to it' at such time as he should come to it again, but really in order to go on not looking at it. Playwrights he had heard or read about sometimes reported difficulty in getting their characters plausibly off the stage. He was all right at that part; with his characters the trouble lay in getting them plausibly on to the stage and finding things, plausible or implausible, for them to say once there. Bowen shook his head and sighed. What he needed was a bloody *theme*. But they didn't grow on trees, did they? No, that was not what they did.

'You're looking fit,' Bennie Hyman said to him when they met.

'Really? That's a comfort. Yes please. One just like you've got.'

'Barbara all right?'

'Yes, full of . . . full of fun.'

'And the kids?'

'Oh, tremendous.'

'Good.' Hyman then talked for ten minutes about how nasty being a bachelor was. It was sincere but failed to grip. When it was over he said: 'Anything new on that trip abroad you were thinking of?'

Bowen gave a throttled cry. 'Yes, lots. We're going all right. Can't get out of it now.' He explained about the American commission. 'See? It's like being deprived of your citizenship.'

'Is it, now? Is it? With finances fixed and a car laid on? You're in a bad way all right. You know what I'm going to say now, don't you? Well, here it is. I wish I could turn it all up and get away abroad for a bit.'

'Ah, but I don't. I like it here, you see. And anyway, it's my mother-in-law's car, you fool. And look, it's just struck me: how do they mean, mother-in-law? What law? What law says she's my mum?'

'I'll explain it to you if you don't watch out. What I don't see is why it shouldn't be your mother-in-law's car. A car can't hurt you, can it? What's wrong with it?'

'As a car, nothing. Only it's her way of reminding me that she's about. Not near necessarily, a thousand miles away perhaps, but about. And she's thought up another way of doing that. She's practically made it a condition of lending us the car that I take dozens of photographs of us abroad and the bits of abroad we see and us looking at them and so on. So she can share it all with us. That's right. So I can feel her breathing down my neck every time I click the shutter. I've even had to promise – and I mean promise – to stick the bloody things in an album as we get them developed so they shan't get lost or damaged or out of

13

order. What about that, eh? It's enough to drive you up the wall.'

'So I see. Decided where you're going yet?'

'It's all the same to me, if you know what I mean.'

'Mm. Well, why not try Portugal, then? Lots of sun, not overrun with Yanks and British, cheap as hell. And the national poet was put on the skids back in the sixteenth century or whenever it was and there's been sod-all since. That should appeal to you?'

'What about that filthy Fascist government?'

'Ah, get stuffed, what's that to you? Give you something to go for in your piece for the New York boys. No, seriously, Garnet, you think it over. Good place, Portugal. An uncle of mine went there a year or two ago and was pissed all the time on about ten bob a day.'

'What about another of those while we're on the subject?'

'No, let's go in.' Hyman got up, revealing himself as ridiculously athletic in figure as well as exaggeratedly Nordic in face. He looked very unlike a successful young publisher. But he was. This fact was familiar enough to Barbara Bowen, and so was the related fact that her husband read an occasional manuscript for the firm. A third fact, that Bowen was trying to get Hyman to get the firm to give him a job, was unknown to her. Bowen had often thought that not getting this job would carry the consolation prize of not having to tell Barbara anything about it. She had a way of viewing regular salaried employment as somehow inimical to integrity. She had said as much pretty often in the first stages of their courtship, less often in the latter stages, not at all for about a year after their marriage, and pretty often again during the seven years after that. Many of her views had described that parabola.

Bowen followed Hyman into the restaurant. It was a

rather expensive one and Hyman always gave you lunch there, whether he was going to try to get you to do something for him, explain that he was not going to do something for you, or just give you lunch. Bowen wondered which sort of Hyman lunch this was going to be. Then he felt he knew.

They were drinking their coffee when Hyman said: 'I suppose you'll be flying over, will you? On your trip, I mean?'

Bowen gave another throttled cry. He remembered very clearly what that climbing turn had felt like the day one of his R.A.F. pals took him up to show him Cader Idris from the air. He decided it would be hard to discriminate the horror-potential of the terms 'plane' and 'immediate mobilization'. Nothing would ever get him into the air, not even a life-contract with the *Times Literary Supplement*. He put this view to his friend.

Hyman sniffed. 'You'll have a long time at sea otherwise.'

'I shan't mind that. But wait a minute: why will I?'

'Lisbon's three days from Southampton, that's all.'

'Oh, I've got to go to Lisbon, have I?'

'No, but there's one thing you can do there that you can't do anywhere else.'

'I'm always game for a new thrill. But I'm taking Barbara along, and it'd be a bit hard to work up an alibi when I . . .'

'Quiet now,' Hyman said, looking round for the waiter. 'I've got something rather interesting to tell you, but you must promise to keep it under your hat. Let's try a little experiment. Wulfstan Strether. What's your reaction?'

'Boredom, chiefly. I never seem to get on with great novelists.'

'Don't you? I can't help thinking I remember a talk on the Third a year or two ago on the twentieth anniversary of *Rapid Falcons* coming out. Or wasn't that you?'

'I'm afraid it was me, but only because old Cyril got ill at the last moment and couldn't do it. I was just filling in to oblige.'

'You fascinate me. Anyway, what do you know about Strether himself, as distinct from his stuff?'

'Nothing at all. I thought that was the whole point about him. But, after all, you published him, didn't you? You must have some dope on him, surely. No point in coming to me.'

'We still do publish him. All five of his novels have been in print ever since the day they first appeared. That's, what, ten years, isn't it? or more, from the last one, which was that, *Mad as the Mist and Snow*?'

'No, *This Rough Magic* was the last one, in '46. Don't you remember all that Prospero stuff at the end about drowning his book? – pity he didn't. And how everybody decided it must mean he was packing it in?'

'Of course,' Hyman said. 'Same again? Go on, it'll do you good. Yes, that's right. And he did pack it in, you see, or so it appeared. Anyway, you know no more than that about the one indisputably major talent to have arisen since the death of Conrad?'

'D. H. Lawrence, you mean. Well, I know the rumours about him really being some industrial magnate, or that he's a bloke in a monastery who can't afford to let the Father Superior know he's been writing novels in the firm's time. Oh, and all that business round about 1950 about him being dead. Was anything ever established about that? You ought to know.'

'Yes, I ought to, oughtn't I? I think all that was based on some more stuff in the *Rough Magic* thing.'

'Entirely based on that, was it?'

'That's another thing I don't know. Listen, I'll put you in the picture, Garnet. All Strether's stuff was handled by old

16

man Hiscock in person. He even used to address Strether's letters and take them to the post himself. Conscientious old bird, Hiscock. Or I suppose you might call him literal-minded. Anyway, Strether wanted his identity kept dark and for Hiscock that meant keeping it dark from everybody, including the other directors and his own wife. It also meant keeping all the contracts and correspondence – both ends of it – locked away. But when Hiscock goes round the corner and we look through his papers, not so much as a bloody twitter do we find about Strether – couple of years ago now, that was, just about the time I got on to the Board. Well, old Hiscock went very suddenly, down at his place in Sussex on Friday night and dead in bed on Sunday morning. He may have felt himself going, not had time to get hold of Strether and ask him what to do about all the stuff, so he burns the lot to be on the safe side. Anyway, we've hunted high and low, boy, believe me. Not a bloody twitter.'

'Yes, I can see it's annoying.'

'Annoying, Christ, I could stand it if it was just annoying, I get all the practice I need. It's far more than that. Ten days ago a typescript turns up in the office, a novel, a long one, about a hundred and twenty thousand, called – I can hardly bring myself to say it – called *One Word More*. See what I'm on about?'

'I'm ahead of you, chum, don't worry. And there's really no way of telling if it's genuine?'

'I've passed it round on the quiet to a couple of chaps. Bad Strether, they say, and I agree with them. Fat lot of use that is. Anybody with the kind of mind that wins the literary competitions in the weeklies, plus the necessary energy, could have done it. So could Strether himself, granted that he's out of practice and a bit past it. And we're completely on our arse when it comes to deciding which it

is, whether it's genuine or not. You can see the little difficulties that that raises.'

'I take it Strether and Hiscock had never met?'

'Too right, sport. There's no way of checking up on this
fellow at all at the moment. Just assume for the sake of
argument that he's a fake. At different times he reads in
the papers, (a) that Hiscock was as close as an oyster about
the Strether business, (b) your point about them never having met, (c) there's a fighting chance that the real Strether's
under the sod, and (d) old Hiscock's death to round it off.
Well then, why not try it on? To a certain kind of mind it'd
be irresistible.'

'A disappointed writer who wants to make fools of the
literary world? Like that Dutch chap who painted the
Vermeers?'

'Could be; I wouldn't know. Anyway, we're all a bit
nervous about it. We've written straight back, of course,
saying how delighted we all are. Always withdraw it later
on if we've got to. We're having another look for the Hiscock dope too, naturally, though I doubt if we'll find anything as late as this. But you see how we're fixed. We don't
want anyone else to publish this thing if it's genuine. On
the other hand we don't want to publish it if it isn't. I say
"we". Speaking for myself I don't think it would matter; we publish enough fakes under their real names as
it is. It's old Weinstein who's a bit edgy about it, and the
others tend to take their time from him. Don't know
whether you remember that book on linguistics we did a
year or two ago, turned out to be a thesis the author had
pinched from some Belgian or Luxemburger or what-have-
you. It's made poor old Weinstein a bit sensitive about
things. You know, a bit niggly. He doesn't want any more
allegations of inefficiency and gullibility and so on for a
few months. There's plenty of time to play with and I'm

sure we can get it all sorted out if we put our minds to it. But what old Weinstein's after just now is someone to go and see the author of *One Word More*, whoever he may be, and probe him, manoeuvre him into producing something that'll clinch things, a letter from Hiscock or a bit of fan-mail or something. I told him we hadn't got to that stage yet. But it would be very interesting if someone could go and see this character and sort of see what the score is, kind of thing. That's where you come in.'

'Do you know,' Bowen said, 'I was expecting me to do that round about here. So whoever it is lives in Portugal, does he? Why can't he live in England like everyone else?'

Hyman glared at him as he signed the bill. 'Still on that one, are you?'

'No, just coming back momentarily to that one. Anyway, as they say, what's in it for me?'

'Well, obviously, if it turns out to be Strether – and personally I'm pretty sure it will – there's an article there you'll be able to name your own price for, once we've given you the go-ahead. In the second place we'll weigh in with your expenses however the business turns out. And then there's that job with us you're after. Things aren't too bright at the moment, but . . .'

'But old Jorkins – I mean old Weinstein might look on me rather more favourably if I do this chore for him, is that it?'

'More or less it, yes. What about it? I thought it might be a bit of fun for you with some financial interest thrown in.'

'But this bloke won't want me charging in, will he, if he's a sort of hermit like they say?'

'Ah, that's all changed now. He knows he won't write anything else now, he says, so he's abandoning secrecy. Hopes to come to London in a year or so. That'll be the day. Mind you, it gives you a place to dig. Ask him why he's changed his line.'

'Yes. But I don't much fancy the idea of spying on him.'

'You know, you're wasted over here, Garnet. Ought to be in the States, giving your integrity the rounds of the advertising world or public relations. You won't be spying, you owl. You're just going to look him up and let me know how he strikes you. Well?'

'All right, provided I can sell Barbara the idea of Portugal.'

'That's your problem, brother. Thank you.' He took his hat and donned it, for they stood now in the foyer. 'As soon as I hear definitely from you I'll get the cheque made out.'

'Oh yes, how much will it be? Twenty-five?'

'Not less than twenty, anyway. Good. We'll have another chat before you go. Right, all the best then, Garnet *bach*. See you.'

'Thanks for the lunch, Bennie. *Mazel tov*.'

Hyman began walking away, then stopped, doubled up, and turned. 'Just the thing for you, this, isn't it? You and your sham-detecting lark. Be nice to see what happens. A sort of test, in a way.'

2

The test that interested Bowen in the next few hours concerned not Strether or pseudo-Strether but the miniature evacuation of his homeland that lay ahead of him. Would he be able to make it? And what would he do all the time if he did, apart from writing his play and hoping not to be addressed in a foreign tongue? He thought of this before, during and after his visit to the offices of a literary journal he sometimes contributed to. The only books he was allowed to take away were a work on the decline of Western culture (800 words by next Thursday), a lavishly-illustrated volume about dinosaurs (for his elder children) and a handsome affair to do with flowers of hedgerow and woodland (for flogging). But he cheered himself up by extracting a promise to print a short article, when the time came, in the journal's 'European Notebook' section. He was now well over a hundred pounds up on the day. A little treat tonight, then.

At his local wine-shop in search of the little treat, he looked with great interest and lurking dread at all the manifestations of abroad that were to be seen around him: France, Italy, Germany, Spain, Algeria, Jamaica, Holland, the Union of South Africa, Poland, Chile – he closed his eyes at the memory of the epilogue to a Chilean-burgundy party last Christmas – Australia, Portugal. Yes, Portugal. Mm. Oh well. It was still rather moving to think of all those citizens of distant lands working so hard to make it possible for him to be drunk here in London. He got a nice Moselle for himself ('rather like a Barsac, sir,' the man said, 'if you know your wines') and some Golden Sweet Malaga and a bottle of pop for his wife. As he walked along to the flat he thought hard about abroad, as he was often to do in the next few weeks.

For someone like him, he reasoned, deportation was a long-standing need. He pleaded with himself that he was getting into a rut and that it was no defence to say that he liked ruts. Everything had gone too easily for him: the first in English at Swansea, the three years on the local rag and at wing-forward for the All-Whites, emigration to London and subbing on the national daily, the last two and a half years freelancing and still on the up-and-up, with even a book behind him. (It was a collection of tarted-up reviews

21

No Dogmas Allowed, and he looked forward to its getting further and further behind him.) Anyway, he had come off pretty well compared with the two other people who had got firsts in his year: richer, freer and working less than poor Menna Talmadge, who was still teaching in the Midlands, and freer than Fred Rogers, who helped to do publicity for a car combine. Yes, Bowen thought, a good shaking-up is what I want? Want? Well, need. Need? Well, ought to have, then.

A children's party of some kind seemed to be going on in the flat when he got to it; at any rate, there was more noise than he could easily imagine his own three making. He therefore went up to his study, a room that deserved the name of 'den' more than most by reason of its hole-like aspect and the remarkable gamey smell coming from the wallpaper. It was on the half-landing and Bowen had established himself in it as a result of an ambiguity in the agreement with the landlord, who lived on the upstairs floor with a person conjectured by Bowen to be his boy-friend. The landlord was of wild appearance, with a lot of scurf on his eyebrows, and gossip at the pub on the corner had it that he was supposed to be a sculptor. The quality and tendency of this supposition was one of the many minor reasons why Bowen disliked being supposed to be a dramatist. Apart from occasional arguments about Bowen's right to the den, he had had no contact with the landlord at all since an evening in the autumn when the fellow, looking wilder than usual, had met him in the street and taken him into a neighbouring back-garden to show him the gridded top of an alleged ventilation shaft from the underground Railway. Later that night the Bowens had heard a two-hour quarrel raging overhead. They had failed to work out what part, if any, was being played in it by the ventilation shaft.

Bowen sat down in the crackling basket-chair and picked up the new Graham Greene. He had nothing against that author either personally or aesthetically, but wished he would die soon so that his lecture on him would not keep on having to have things added to it every eighteen months or so. Perhaps it would be better in the long run to set his teeth and make the switch to E. M. Forster. The new Graham Greene, like most of the old Graham Greenes, was about abroad. Extraordinary how the region kept coming up. There must be something in it: not all the people who thought so were horrible. A couple of months there would be like learning to drive or making a determined start on *Finnegans Wake* – an experience bound in itself to be arduous and irritating, but one which could conceivably render available a rich variety of further experiences. And he knew he would never have taken such a step voluntarily; it had taken a team made up of Barbara, Barbara's mother and the staff of *See* Magazine, with Bennie Hyman as first reserve, to bring him to this point.

Bowen told himself that he suffered from acute prejudice about abroad. Some of this he thought he recognized as unreasonable, based as it was on disinclination for change, dislike of fixing up complicated arrangements, and fear of making a fool of himself. One of his many archetypal images of abroad was of a man inquiring about his luggage in dumb-show while a queue formed behind him – except that of course it wouldn't be a queue there, but a pushing, jostling crowd. Further, he fancied that he had a long history of lower-middle-class envy directed against the upper-middle-class traveller who handled foreign railway-officials with insolent ease, discussed the political situation with the taxi-driver in fluent *argot*, and landed up first go at exactly the right hotel, if indeed he wasn't staying with some *contessa*, all cigarette-holder and *chaise-longue*, who called him by a foreign version of his christian name. He tried it over : Garnetto, Garnay, or rather Guhghr-nay. Later, he mused, they went off and dined, exquisitely and *madly* cheaply, at – that's right, a little place one or other of them happened to know about, where – yes, you could get the best *merluza rellena al estilo de toro* in Valencia.

He was musing about what happened when they got back from the little place when his wife came in with a tray. It had their tea on it. Seeing the notes and open book on his lap, the pencil in his hand, she asked with just a dash of incredulity in her childish tones : 'Are you busy, darling?'

'Oh no, I haven't really settled down yet. Had a good day?'

'Fair to middling, you know. How was Bennie?'

'Oh, fine. Damn' good lunch, as always.'

'What did he want out of you this time? More sweated manuscript-reading?'

Bowen arranged his mug and plate carefully before replying. He would have to go slowly about the Strether project, release only some of the details now and those a bit at a time, allow the idea to merge into the unregarded furniture of her mind. Otherwise she would get excited one way or the other. Either she would stand over him until and while he wrote to Strether announcing their arrival and offering to bring with them any books, periodicals and general stores he might want, or she would stand over him until and while he rang up Bennie Hyman and told him that, for reasons in some way involving integrity, the deal was off. In a tone which he tried to make sound merely bored, but which in fact suggested a statement made during an interval of the *peine forte et dure*, he said : 'Well ... there wasn't really ... very much ... worth mentioning.

I told him our trip was definitely on, and we discussed that ...'

'I suppose he suggested Monte Carlo or somewhere, did he?'

'No, he ... no, he seemed to think Portugal might be a good bet. He'd heard quite good reports of it, apparently: cheap, you know, and not too ... Whatever's the matter, dear?'

Barbara's already large eyes had dilated considerably, so that a good deal of white was visible under each pupil. The fact that she had her mouth full of swiss roll and was chewing it vigorously, a normal enough proceeding in itself, made the eye-business rather alarming. 'This is extraordinary,' she said, blowing out crumbs.

'What is? Are you all right?'

'I had lunch with Olivia.'

'What a good idea.'

'You know, it really seems as if things are arranging themselves in a very queer way. By the time I left her' – she paused, for effect or to lick her fingers – 'I'd more or less made up my mind, subject to your approval of course ... that Portugal was where we ought to go.'

'What a funny thing.'

'It's more than that, darling. It's obviously what we're intended to do, what life's got in store for us. There's obviously some reason behind it we shan't know till we get there. Don't you see? It's the next thing to happen to us.'

Bowen lit one of the small Dutch cigars he treated himself to at prosperous periods. He disguised a long sigh as a long exhalation of smoke. Barbara was being mystical again, another habit that, after a few months' recession around the time of their marriage, was booming these days with all its pristine vigour. It had no basis in religion or even in superstition as it is ordinarily thought of; it had no truck with anything as tangible as stopped clocks, dreams or unlikely coincidences. Ordinary run-of-the-mill coincidences, such as this Portugal one, were what usually set her off. Bowen had often asked himself what she really thought she meant by this contemporary-style occultism, and in the early days had asked her as well. No good, though. Any reluctance on his part to accept her auguries was likely to earn him a smiling, raised-eyebrow rebuke for surrendering to market-place obtuseness. He cheered up again now as he recognized that at least Portugal would need no selling to Barbara after this; his aim henceforth must be to stop her from trying to arrive there by first light in the morning.

Barbara developed her theme for a minute or two, then suddenly became practical. She was good at being that, much better than he, which was how she got away with being also better at being spiritual than he. 'Olivia was telling me,' she said with the ingenuous vivacity that had first attracted him to her, 'that the A.A. do it all. I'll go and see them in the morning and get the details. They even put the car on the ship for you.'

'They do, do they? Who takes it off again?'

'Oh, they arrange for a foreign A.A. chap to meet you.'

Many years previously Bowen had read a programme note, rather emotionally worded, on the Sixth Symphony of Tchaikovsky – the old *Pathétique*. After some talk about the note of hectic defiance to be remarked in the third movement, the writer had characterized the finale as *the utterance of a soul stricken by doubt, horror and despair.* This little triad later came to fit exactly the state of Bowen's soul when confronted with what he saw as the basic abroad-situations: those involving policemen, waiters, beggars, hotel clerks, drunks, madwomen, Customs officers, porters, ferry supervisors, car-park attendants and persons who had perforce to be asked the way to the nearest lavatory. As he puffed his Dutch cigar that day a sample version of doubt, horror and despair gave the ulceration of his duodenum a nudge forward at the thought of conversing with, or more likely remarking the absence of, the foreign A.A. chap. 'That's a comfort,' he said.

'Evidently Olivia's in-laws have got a pal in Lisbon who might help us to get fixed up. She's going to ask them.'

'What sort of pal?'

'Oh, quite an important pal, I gather. The bits of Lisbon he doesn't own are more or less not worth having. You know Olivia.'

Bowen did, and said so. The wife of a man who was just stopping being supposed to be an architect and starting being an architect, she used to smile at Bowen sometimes in a way that seemed to point out the impracticability of her ever yielding to his desires, natural enough and even creditable as these were. At other times, though less often since her husband had been given a half-share in doing that infants' school at Penge, her demeanour suggested moral revolt at the whole concept of Bowen's fitness to perform the sexual act. Bowen viewed these demonstrations kindly; after all, he reasoned, the forty per cent more chin which might imaginably entitle her to them would also render them unnecessary to her.

'Still, it'll probably be jolly useful, darling. He can probably get us a villa just by clicking his fingers. And we shan't be committing ourselves to anything just by letting him help us. One visit to thank him for what he's done and then we needn't see any more of him.'

'Exactly,' Bowen said, smiling at her. Both word and smile derived from how he had begun to feel about Portugal.

Quite apart from the matter of the Lisbon pal and his finger-licking potentialities, there was the business about Britain's oldest ally and the fact that port came from there. It was true that a recent article had named Portugal as the least jazz-conscious country in Europe, but against this could be set something he had once read about everyone there not liking the Spaniards. Good stuff. Bowen felt this to be so even though he thought he recognized intellectually that the Spaniards couldn't possibly be as bad as the impression of them to be gained from those who lauded them in print, and even though individual Spaniards he had heard of seemed amiable enough — Cervantes, Picasso, Casals and the man who had lent a pair of trousers to a friend of Bowen's who had been locked out of his flat in his dressing-gown. The lender of trousers had been flying to Madrid the next morning, too. A real *hidalgo*, that one.

Barbara lit one of her small filter-tipped cigarettes and tucked her legs up under her on the lopsided couch. If some of her ideas could seem unduly self-conscious, her physical demeanour never was. She began talking enthusiastically and vaguely, the black plume of her ponytail hair-do tossing to and fro, about how they would get to Portugal and what they would do once there. Bowen watched her contentedly, rather drowsily too: Hyman's lunch, its effects delayed by his afternoon visits, was heavy upon him. He thought what a nice wife he had, and that she would be perfect if she would only take him as she found him, a form of treatment he had long since begun meting out to her. Excess of energy was really her trouble: you could tell a lot from the fact that when she waved her hand to people, as she was always doing, she waved it from the shoulder instead of the wrist, and that when she stirred a pan on the stove she waggled her bottom to the same rhythm — not that he minded that at all. These days her manner to him was one of affectionate banter, lively demon-. stration of fondness for him which was increasingly accompanied by resolute concern to get him smartened up. Her rehabilitation programme had so far been directed only at the outworks of his personality: clothes, hours, drinking procedures, finance, the institution of a warning system to deal with the sudden cancellations and rearrangements he said his freelance status made necessary. For quite a time he had had no cause to revise his private imitation of how she put her head on one side and stared at his hairbrush before taking it off to wash it, nor the one of how she brightened her tone, like someone reading to a very young or very old invalid, whenever she came out with something like 'He sounded a bit het-up over the phone but I told him I was quite certain you were working on it and would get it to him in time.' She was far from being always like that, and going to bed with all that slender brunette beauty continued to be both emotionally edifying and unbeatable fun – as if the *Iliad* or some other gruelling cultural monument had turned out to be a good read as well as a masterpiece. Fine. But what would happen when she stopped tinkering with his habits and moved inwards to the bedraggled sprawl that was the core of his being? He sometimes thought that the key to her, and also the key to the much more puzzling problem of what she saw in him, was that being his wife gave her something to get her teeth into. She was a connubial worker in the way that some people were social workers.

But meditating in this haphazard fashion would not do. Already his silence might have been taken as assent to some proposal that he should cable the British Council in Lisbon or take over, for the duration, the task of giving Sandra her midnight bottles. He said: 'It'll be interesting to see what abroad's really like.'

'Darling, isn't that what I keep *telling* you? You can't live on your prejudices for ever, you know.'

'Oh yes I can. Of course, I know envy's tied up a lot with the way we feel about it.'

'You mean the way *you* feel about it.'

'Still, you know, you take Olivia. You look at the way she goes on about abroad. Not really very creditable. There's a lot like her. They go on about it – it's like old Binns at the pub telling you how bloody marvellous his new house is going to be. Sort of boasting.'

'Little article there, Bowen, I can tell.'

'You can't go on about how well you know London – that's provincial – but you can go on about how well you know abroad. In print, too. Suppose you're reviewing a novel with an Italian background. You can't just say you think it's well done, especially if you're a bloody woman. No, honestly, dear. "Mr Shagbag has caught to perfection the atmosphere of those precipitous little streets that run up from the Rua Latrina to the Palazzo del ... Allegro non Troppo." In other words I've got some service in too, see? And, Christ, people like that – just a minute, dear – people like that are the very ones who'd turn up their noses if some poor sod in a pub says, you know, "Excuse me but I couldn't help overhearing what you were saying about Naples – I had a pretty sticky time there in '43" or whenever it was, oh Christ.'

'I wish you'd write this sort of thing down instead of just telling me about it. You really should ...'

'Not worth it. Anyway I'll remember it. Of course, I don't mind the chaps who more or less have to live there, health reasons or money or job or ...'

'Jolly good of you.'

'You take all these homos, now ...'

'Darling, you really don't have to convince me that

you're not a jessie. Wouldn't be a bad idea if you were a bit of a one, then perhaps you wouldn't goggle so hard at every pair of . . .'

'All right, fair enough, but all I'm talking about, you can't blame them, the laws being what they are, but the way they go on sometimes, like a student saying "Look at me. I drink beer. I smoke. I speak to girls. Look at me, then." When they work that in with the abroad thing it makes you bloody sweat, man. All that stuff about the land of the delicate olive. Here, did I sing you that bit John and I made up the other evening? Goes to the tune of *Come Where the Booze is Cheaper*? Did I?'

'Yes, you sang it about eight times after you got in.'

'No, that was the new Jack Jones verse about my sister's a keen chapel-goer. This one goes:

> Come where the . . .'

'Charming, I'm sure.'

'Wait a minute –

> . . . cheaper,
> Come to the Southern shore,
> Cradle of all our values,
> Where the boys hang round your door;
> Land of the vine and olive . . .

– that's what reminded me of it –'

> They'll never tell your mum;
> For a packet of fags they just pull . . .'

'Darling, I love this sort of thing, as you know, but the kids are just outside, playing on the stairs, and it's not . . .'

'All right, dear. Anyway, where was I? Yes, and all that stuff about the spirit being chilled and restricted in the foggy atmosphere of Anglo-Saxon provincialism. Anglo-

Saxon policemen, they mean. Why can't they say what they mean? Then there are the chaps who are simply bloody fools, but I don't mind them so much. You remember Leslie Evans after his year in Paris? – "you're much freer there, you know." Yeah, that's right. They shrug their shoulders or whatever it is they do and mutter about mad Englishmen instead of kicking you up the behind. Mind you, I feel sorry for anybody who's as big a bloody fool as poor old Les. But I wish he wouldn't think he'd got the right to knock the English. That's what really gets on my wick.'

Barbara gave him one of her charming smiles as he fell grudgingly silent. It was partly intended, he knew, to indicate that he must be aware of several weaknesses in his tirade, but that she loved him too much, and respected his intelligence too much, to point them out. The fact that it remained a charming smile when all this was subtracted from it was an impressive tribute to something or other. She gathered up the tea things. 'We'll talk about Portugal again at dinner-time,' she said. 'Oh, isn't it lovely?'

'I brought some Malaga and pop in for you.'

'Oh, you marvellous boy.'

Currency bum, Bowen thought to himself when she had gone. Allowance for self, wife, three children and car bum. Arrangements for drafts on foreign banks bum. Steamer tickets bum. Return vouchers bum. Car documents bum. Redirection of correspondence *by landlord* bum. Permission from Secretary of Extra-Mural Studies to absent self from end-of-session Tutors' and Lecturers' Discussion and Planning Meeting bum. Passport bum. Passport photograph bum. Visa bum.

As an alternative to this he picked up his Graham Greene notes. Crossing out a mention of *The End of the Affair* which stood above an already-cancelled mention of *The*

Heart of the Matter, he amended a sentence to read: '*The Quiet American* shows every sign of marking a transition in Mr Greene's development as a novelist.'

3

'Dad.'

'Yes?'

'How big's the boat that's taking us to Portugal?'

'I don't know really. Pretty big, I should think.'

'As big as a killer whale?'

'What? Oh yes, easily.'

'As big as a blue whale?'

'Yes, of course, as big as any kind of whale.'

'Bigger?'

'Yes, much bigger.'

'How much bigger?'

'Never you mind how much bigger. Just bigger is all I can tell you. Isn't there a comic there you can read?'

'Mark's reading the only one I haven't read.'

'Mark, can you give David that comic and read another for a bit? That one's the only one he hasn't read.'

'It's the only one I haven't read too, Dad.'

'Any case, I don't want to read, I want to chat, Dad.'

'Oh, God.'

'Dad.'

'Yes?'

'If two tigers jumped on a blue whale, could they kill it?'

'Ah, but that couldn't happen, you see. If the whale was in the sea the tigers would drown straight away, and if the whale was . . .'

'But supposing they did jump on the whale?'

'. . . on land it would die very soon anyway, I think I'm right in saying. Or perhaps it'd be dead already. Yes, I think it'd have to be, to be on land. Anyway, it couldn't happen.'

'But supposing it did?'

'Oh, God. Well, I suppose the tigers'd kill the whale eventually, but it'd take a long time.'

'How long would it take one tiger?'

'Even longer. Now I'm not answering any more questions about whales or tigers.'

'Dad.'

'Oh, what is it now, David?'

'If two sea-serpents . . .'

Bowen now forbade his elder son all speech under penalty of physical mutilation. A waiver in cases of imminent excretion or vomiting was petitioned for and allowed, but only because all five Bowens were travelling by car at the time. Barbara drove it with concentration and skill, even with a certain dash, punctiliously making with the hand-signals, giving buses right of way, tooting a warning to just the kind of child who might suddenly dash across the road. She also drove in complete silence.

Currency bum, tickets bum and other stray posteriors had been satisfactorily, even creditably, dispatched. Passport photograph nates had given Bowen a chance to behave like a Somerset Maugham character by comparing his new one with the one he had had taken for his only previous civilian trip abroad in 1946. A party that included Barbara, at that time not yet Bowen's wife (in fact the young lady of someone quite different), had spent three weeks at Remiremont, Vosges, largely because it was the only place in France any of them had heard of outside the realms of history, geography and gossip columns. The food had been good and Bowen had had his hair cut in the village just as if he was French himself.

34

The comparison of the portraits had been of value and interest. The lad in the 1946 one had looked back at Bowen with petulant, head-on-one-side sensitivity. Wearing a nasty suit, he had seemed on the point of asking Bowen why he wasn't a pacifist or what he thought of *Aaron's Rod*. The 1956 Bowen was twice as wide and had something of the air of a television panellist. His question about *Aaron's Rod* would have concerned how much money whoever wrote it had made out of it. It was odd how the two of them could differ so much and yet both look exactly the kind of man he would most dislike to meet or be.

Barbara, on the evidence presented, had changed from the kind of fourteen-year-old one might expect to find hiding in a U.S. Army barrack-room to the kind of concentration-camp wardress who had lampshades made of human skin. The knowledge that this was not so had helped to reconcile Bowen to the petulant sensitive and the television panellist. But both were warnings.

Despite the help he had had, mainly from Bennie Hyman, fixing up the trip had given Bowen much more to do than he had expected even when he had thought he was going to have to do everything himself. Packing bum, *accountant* bum (including arrangements for payment of income-tax demand *buttock*), special shopping expeditions (aaoh! aoh! aooh!) bum, and labelling bum (especially that) had all taken their toll. Still, they were now adequately prepared, all the way from the mosquito-repellent – with mosquito-bite ointment in case the outer defences should fall – to completed negotiations for drafts on a Portuguese bank. This bank had given Bowen his only laugh for several weeks by being called the *Banco Spirito Santo e Comercial de Lisboa*, a synthesis of God and Mammon as arresting as any feature of the Anglo-Saxon Christmas.

· In a much longer time than it takes to tell the Bowens had got to Southampton, found the right dock after two or three tours of that part of the county, waited long enough there for both boys to ask almost continuously to be taken back to South Kensington and for Sandra to fall off a bench on to her face, gone on board and been directed to their cabin. The ship seemed nice at a first look but proportioned rather on the lines of an Indian war canoe. Bowen mentioned this to Barbara.

'How do you mean?' she said.

'Well, I mean it's narrow, that's all.'

'Oh, I see. Will it matter, do you think?'

'It might, I suppose. I wouldn't know really.' Bowen thought briefly about the Bay of Biscay, then at more length about the Derry-Brown Stabilizers he had read about in the shipping-company brochure. There had been a diagram of them.

In their cabin they found Bennie Hyman, surrounded by their luggage and drinking a large gin and tonic. Before speaking he pressed the bell at his side. Then he greeted them heartily. Barbara responded less heartily but still fairly heartily. Bowen was delighted, but a little suspicious at the same time. He said: 'Christ, it's good of you to come all this way, Bennie. What is it, seventy miles?'

'Not quite — I was weekending with some people in Winchester, so I thought I might as well pop down and see you safely away on the billow. I got a glimpse of you on the dock, but I thought I couldn't do any good there, especially not for myself, so I argued my way along here and drank. Feeling a bit pissed now as a matter of fact. Watch out I'm not still here when she sails. Everything gone off all right?'

'Yes, thanks to you, boy.'

'Ah —' He glanced over at Barbara, who was opening

36

some telegrams, and continued: 'Nonsense, chumbo. A pleasure. I can tell you're wondering why I'm really here. Well, I'm really here for the same reason I seem to be here ... *Christ.*' He pressed the bell again. 'Yes, I'm just seeing you off. I know you think I'm a pretty devious sort of character. You're wrong for once, though. Brought you one or two things which I'll give you while I can still remember. Letter of introduction to old Buckmaster – that's what we call the old man of mystery in the office, tired of going on about the chap who says he's Strether all the time, too much of a rigmarole.'

'Why Buckmaster?'

'That was me, actually. Just a name I happened to spot once on one of those corset and jock-strap shops, you know the kind of thing. I thought it was bloody funny. Ah, here we are. Things always turn up in the end if you wait long enough. Now what are we all going to have? Barbara?'

While drinks were ordered Bowen read the telegrams. There was a Greetings one and an ordinary one. The ordinary one said: HAVE G OOD TRIP DEADLINE WAUGH PIECE NINTH AT LATEST SEND AIRMAIL REGARDS + HEWSON. The Greetings one said: ALL MY LOVE GOE SWITH YOU MY FARLINGS SEND ALL NEWS AND KEEP PHOTOGRAPHAL BUM TO SHOW ON RETURN BON VOYAGE + MOTHER. There is a God, Bowen thought. He broke into violent coughing while Barbara watched him suspiciously. 'Mother' was of course her mother. She was called Mrs Knowles.

Hyman said: 'And here's a proof of *One Turd More*. If you let it out of your possession I'll swing on your ... I'll be very cross with you. Oh yes: I've brought you a copy of *This Rough Magic* as well, in case you feel like a spot of analysis and comparison.'

Bowen made faces to try and shut Hyman up. Barbara knew about Strether now, but only as a writer they might visit. Just then she went round the corner of the cabin into the long corridor-like bit that ended at the washbasin and porthole. She carried a wet nappy.

Hyman was going on : 'They should leak it to the papers, just say a new Strether's on the way. It'd flush the real bloke if he's still alive. But Weinstein won't play. Gone into a sort of nervous decline. Can't blame him. It's his can if we publish a smelly one.'

Barbara reappeared. Bowen hoped he was in the clear. Just then an over-amplified voice bawled an instruction about passports. This was followed, with slightly brutal relish he thought, by some business about *os senhores e as senhoras os passageiros*. Already, Bowen said to himself. A few minutes later Hyman asked to go up on deck, where he said there might be some more air. There proved to be a great deal more, all of it moving fast and very cold. Barbara had stayed in the cabin to see to the children, each of whom Hyman presented with some money. He had hung about for a moment as if assessing whether or not to kiss Barbara, but had just said good-bye after all.

'Sod this,' he said, shivering. 'Hope it'll be warmer where you're going. But of course it will. Practically tropical. You'll come back with a rich tan and the air of one whom life's colourful pageant has not passed by.'

It was Bowen's concern to come back with a whole rather than a brown skin, and life's colourful pageant would best oblige him by continuing to pass him by. 'You bet,' he said.

'Look, Garnet, what I did want to say to you – don't worry too much about this Buckmaster business. You're going on holiday, after all. I don't want you to feel you've got to give us an answer or anything like that. Can't expect you to. So just enjoy yourself. And, God, I nearly forgot: if you want a life-line, go and call on our agent in Lisbon. I've written him a letter and there's a copy in with the Buckmaster one. Well, fellow, this looks like it. Have a good time. Keep in touch. Don't take any wooden *pesetas* or whatever the bloody things are, and watch it with the local talent. So long, Taff.'

'Cheers, you old shyster. And thanks for everything.'

Hyman reappeared for an instant on the dock, made signs of farewell and then ran out of sight again at a great rate. Bowen thought enviously of the other's leisurely drive back to beautiful London.

Five dark persons, who he noted with idle surprise were all the same height, stood nearby talking simultaneously in a foreign tongue. A loudspeaker added to the din in the same or a related tongue. The increasing Latinity of his surroundings made Bowen feel fretful. Why was abroad occupied exclusively by the Romance-speaking family of nations, with a few Greeks and southern Slavs thrown in? Why was it that Germany, the Low Countries, Scandinavia and the non-southerly Slav areas didn't really count as abroad? Why was it only Frenchmen and Spaniards who got written up as knowing better than the British did 'how to live'? – it was sometimes said of the Dutch too, but that only meant they knew how to look after themselves when it came to eating, drinking and smoking. Why was it that when a chap announced a year's business posting to Rome or Athens, say, people told him how lucky he was, but if he was off to Oslo, Rotterdam or Bremen, people only told the poor sod that it should be 'very interesting', i.e. mind-erodingly boring? Perhaps it was all to do with architecture. Oh, how he loathed architecture. He would have liked to see it all done away with.

These and kindred enigmas occupied him until it was

39

time for him to be having a look at the last of England. There are some moments, it occurred to him, that no amount of dramatization can quite purge of drama. This was one, even though the drama was a trifle more self-regarding than it commonly was, or was acknowledged to be. *Self-exiled Harold wanders forth again*, he thought to himself without really meaning to, *with nought of hope left, but with less of gloom*. (He excused himself for falling a victim to intimations of culture by remembering that his last reading of Byron had been aimed at eking out his review of a new biography, and thus could not fairly be classed as voluntary.) *With less of gloom* ... Well, that overdid things rather, though it was true that Bennie's visit had bucked him up no end, and that duty-free bar prices were still a virgin field of research, a whole new world.

The point where Bowen felt he parted company with self-exiled Harold was in the latter's assertion that *where roll'd the ocean, thereon was his home*. Reluctantly, Bowen looked at the ocean. Even at this stage there was a fair quantity of it, and clearly there was plenty more to come, going down a long way as well as spreading out a long way. The rail on which he was trying to bring himself to lean had one other rung below the top one and an upright every here and there. It was a rail up which sixteen-month-old Sandra would very likely climb if she got the chance. Bowen drew a deep shuddering breath, an action he was to repeat at every recurrence of this image.

Some time after all five Bowens were safely back in England he happened to mention the business to his wife. She said it had worried her too, but she had worked out that, since everybody came up three times before they drowned, she would have been able to get to Sandra at her first, or certainly at her second, reappearance. She had done life-saving with full-size people, so keeping a small child afloat would have given her little difficulty. She did not mention the only reality in her scheme: that in that situation nothing could have stopped her jumping overboard.

Her explanation caused a sort of conditional and retrospective vertigo to seize him. Uttering a snuffling cry, he felt sweat starting out on a brow already amply bedewed at the thought of the television interview with Iris Murdoch he was to conduct later that evening. A car, he reflected when next he was able to, will kill people as surely as drowning; so will a simple domestic accident. But these possibilities did not terrify, they merely incited the taking of precautions. It was the unfamiliarity and the mere size of the surroundings that magnified reactions. He conceived a new respect for the occupants of the *Mayflower* (by all accounts a far less stable ship that the ones currently on the Portugal run), especially for those who took their families with them.

Standing now at the rail, Bowen was asked, in a civil but halting manner, whether that was please the Isle of Wight. He replied that he thought it was, but was not sure. In fact he had no grounds even for supposition. Realizing this abashed and mortified him in some way. The clamour of what he recognized as French and what must be either Spanish or Portuguese or both was increasing as more and more of his fellow-passengers finished settling in and came on deck. He noticed that quite small children were speaking one or other of these languages, and getting results by doing so. One of them, a boy of about nine and of unjustifiable appearance, was looking at him. He decided to go and see how Barbara was getting on, and then to find out the score on this three-mile limit thing.

4

When the boat put in at Cherbourg Bowen was sitting in the lounge, drunkenly trying to read *This Rough Magic*. He had got to page 188, by which time it seemed that the author had gone some way towards finding out what initial situation he proposed to deal with. Those involved were an old painter who was doing a lot of wondering about whether he ought to stop painting now that he considered he was getting much worse at painting, his wife who was frequently described as passionate without it being revealed what she was passionate about or at, and a young man with doe-like eyes who was hanging round the other pair. There was much uncertainty as to whether the young man was interested in the wife or the husband and, if the latter, as to exactly what his focus of interest was. It was uncertain whether this uncertainty existed in the mind of the painter (through whose eyes the action, what there was of it, was viewed) or in that of the young man, or perhaps – the evidence was piling up that way – in that of the author. The first two chapters had been enlivened by the presence of a successful actor, whose person, dress, demeanour, habits, house, father and grandfather had all been conscientiously described, and who now, after talking a good deal about the theatre (that at any rate, Bowen reflected, was well observed), had disappeared from the story, never to return, as far as could be judged from a quick look through the pages that remained.

Bowen yawned. Barbara and the children had been in bed for quite a time. The thought of that cabin, with luggage and children's effects filling such space as was unoccupied by the bunks and Sandra's cot, decided him to get a bit tireder and drunker before joining them. He looked out of the window at what could be seen of France: a bit of wall, a drum or tub of something, a van. But this appearance of inertia did not deceive him. He knew that they were all there really, all on duty demonstrating to one another their capacity for logic, their wit and grace, their responsible and informed interest in politics, their high regard for Poe and Charles Morgan. God, yes...

His mind drifted back to the time when he had been too hard up to resist an invitation to Birmingham, where some foreign persons needed to be addressed on CONTEMPORARY BRITISH NOVELISTS (vi): *Graham Greene.* There was a brief prelude in an underground canteen with fluorescent-strip lighting and lino; the coffee was the prescriptive liquorice with a lacing of varnish. Surrounded by blue-eyed, tanned young men in open-necked shirts, slim-waisted girls with white blouses and no make-up, and a selection of middle-aged bit-players from French films, he felt several times like apologizing for the inroads which both décor and victuals must be making upon these sensitive continental psyches. But they all chattered away gaily, even a little loudly, throwing down the horrible draught with abandon and stubbing out their cigarettes on the barbaric wooden tables in a spirit of careless ease. Two of them had addressed him in English, and he had answered them, for he saw it as his duty to help foreign guests practise being in Great Britain. The only bad moment came on the way upstairs, when he caught sight of a figure in priest's garb and 'Christ, a Jesuit' was his panicked thought. But a snatch of Dublin drollery, audible an instant later, calmed him.

The lecture was all right. After it there was talk of the views, the attitudes, the obsessions, the values of Grim-Grin. One question seemed at first to relate to the face of

Grim-Grin, and he was at a loss to frame an answer until they all assured him that the fellow was really on about the faith of Grim-Grin. Bowen gave them the treatment on that. Then a woman with a lot of beads said:

'We have been hearing of your Grim-Grin and his *Power and the Glory*.'

He agreed that this was the fact.

'But we have been surprised that we have not been hearing of your Edge-Crown.'

'Oh, really?' He searched his brain frantically. Grim-Grin he had been ready for, together with Ifflen-Voff, Zumzit-Mum and Shem-Shoice. This was new. 'Could you amplify that a little?' He ran through the possible variants – Adj-, Ash-, Each-, Age- . . . Some foreigner? But no; it had been *his* Edge-Crown.

'Sickies of sickingdom,' the woman explained irritably.

'Yes . . . of course . . . Well . . .' He began nodding his head with little hope of ever having reason to stop.

After a brief explanatory uproar he was enabled to wonder aloud what had led his questioner to detect a resemblance between *The Power and the Glory* and *The Keys of the Kingdom*, by A. J. Cronin. 'I think I've done enough talking for a bit,' he added, smiling hard and turning his face slowly to and fro for everyone to see, in the hope of suggesting that he was not to be taken altogether seriously. 'Perhaps one of you would like to have a shot at that.'

One of them at once did, saying in a baritone growl: 'There is a priest in both.'

He had got out of it somehow. He had pondered occasionally ever since whether that brilliant Fluellen allusion, given added sting by his own Welshness, had been meant to deride his stupidity or that of the woman with the beads. But of course the point of the experience was not that, nor did it merely illustrate the fact, sadly neglected of recent years, that foreigners talked funny. What life had been trying to say (as Barbara would express it) emerged rather more clearly from the query put to him in excellent English after the lecture: would he please name some of the more important English critical works on A. J. Cronin. (He had got out of that one, too.) Yes, the way the French went overboard about chaps like old Cronin – nothing much wrong with him on another level – did seem a sort of minor national madness, one which gravely damaged their claim to be running European civilization. At least the English never made such howlers. They judged a foreign writer on the basis of the amount of fuss made about him by the foreign Press, or by the writer himself. The latter kind of authority was the one they followed in judging their own writers, so there was consistency there. Well, good luck to them, Bowen thought, in their stout efforts to find Gide and Mauriac worth reading.

He glanced up to find a man watching him. This man was small, elderly and ferocious-looking. He said in a hoarse, American-accented voice: 'You British?'

'Yes.'

'Thought so. Mind if I sit here?'

'Not in the least. Would you like a drink?'

'Thank you, in a little while. We just got on board.'

'Oh yes? On holiday?'

'Well, I don't know as you could call it a holiday exactly. We're never going there again, I do know that.'

'You mean to France?'

'Sure, France, that's what I mean, France. You know France?'

'Not well, no.'

The American leaned closer and began talking rapidly and with few variations of pitch. 'Madeira where we're going is bad enough in all conscience, but by God you almost begin to appreciate a place like that when you get up in this part of the world. There's only one thing they're interested in hereabouts and that's your money. They make no secret of it, I'll give them that. Yes, I'll say that for them, they leave you in no doubt on that score. Gimme gimme gimme, that's their theme song. I thought the Spaniards were on top in that league, but by God these French have certainly got 'em whipped. Take the service in these hotels of theirs. They're so understaffed they're run off their feet – they're exhausted, absolutely exhausted. But if the management try to take on more staff they won't have it, they walk out. Why? Because they'd have to split their tips more ways, that's why. And this Algeria business and the Reds gaining all the time. Ah, the whole country's falling to pieces, it just can't hold up much longer. Not that they don't deserve it; hell, they deserve it all right.'

Bowen was conscious of feeling slightly nettled. If the French were going to be knocked, he felt, he would do the knocking himself, and on ground of his own choosing, on literature or politics, where it didn't matter. 'How do you make that out?'

'I'm telling you, young fellow. But then let me tell you France isn't alone in falling to pieces, no indeed, it's very far from alone in that. You show me one country that isn't falling to pieces, that's all I ask. You'll find it tough, I'm warning you, because I've seen more of the world than you. I was employed in the United States Consular Service and my duties took me to a dozen places in both hemispheres and I never want to see any of them again. I've been retired nearly twelve years now and do you know what we've been doing since then? We've been touring the world – but literally touring the world – looking for some place where we could stand it. We tried South America: nothing but squalor and greed and corruption and ... and sheer

46

horror. We lasted three days in Australia, just three days: dirt and drunkenness and stink everywhere.' He broke off to light a long thin cigar and to cough.

'What about the States? Surely there must be ...'

'Have you ever been to the States, young fellow? Have you seen Americans in their natural habitat? Then let me tell you that they're the most ignorant, vulgar, immoral, godless, materialist, greedy, avaricious, small-minded people on the whole face of this earth. And I ought to know. Life in America today is sheer ... unmitigated ... hell. Only satisfaction is it can't last much longer. It's on the way out. Finished. Doomed. I know what I'm talking about. I give it twenty years at the outside. More like ten in all probability. I'm sorry in a way I shan't be here to see it. But it'll come. And then will you fellows in Europe feel the draught. We make all your goods for you and then give you the money to pay for them. When the States goes you'll just rot away. You're British, aren't you? Then have a drink. Have one with me. You could use one. You may not feel you could, but by God you could. You ... certainly ... could. If you're British as you say, then, boy, could ... you ... use ... a drink.'

British or not, Bowen could, and felt he could too. His companion pressed the bell for a minute or so, looking frequently over his shoulder to make sure Bowen had not stirred. Without consultation he ordered two large Scotches. Then he said: 'The world today is inhabited by a race of sub-men. I'm beginning to see there's only one thing to be done about it. Cut yourself off from it. Fast. While there's still time. And I think I've found the place.'

'Outer Mongolia?'

'Certainly not. In England, oddly enough. The British are the laziest people on the whole face of this earth, but by God you almost begin to appreciate it when it's gimme,

gimme, gimme everywhere else. You know Gloucestershire?'

'Well, I know where it is.'

'You do?' The American sounded sceptical. 'There's a little place called Lydney in Gloucestershire. There's a house near there I can get if I want it. I haven't seen it but my wife has. It's away off on its own. We figured we could hire a man to shop for us and then we wouldn't need to talk to anyone but him. I don't know, but I think it would work. I think it would.'

Bowen put on an intent, earnest look. 'Let's see, now ... Lydney ...'

'You know it?'

'I've been through it a few times. Mm ... No, I don't think I should advise Lydney.'

'What's that to me? You've only been through it. You don't know it, do you? You want water?'

'Yes, please, up to the top ... No, it's too near Wales. Why, it can't be more than ten miles or so from Monmouth.'

'So what?'

'Well, I suppose I'll have to tell you ... Have you ever heard of the Welsh Nationalist Party?'

'No, I haven't. What of it?'

'I didn't think you would have done. Very few people have, outside Wales itself. That's the really frightening thing.'

'You come from Wales? You ... Welsh?'

'Good Lord, no. English to the backbone, thank God.'

'Well ... just what are you talking about?'

'Now very little of this gets into the English papers, you see. Of course, there are Welshmen all over England in positions of power, especially in London. A lot of key posts in the administration have been infiltrated by Welshmen. Oh, they're a clever lot, you've got to hand it to them. I've seen them at work.'

'I still don't get you, young fellow.'

Bowen took his time lighting one of his Dutch cigars. 'The Welsh Nationalist Party,' he said, gesturing, 'is a revolutionary party. So far there hasn't been very much activity out in the open – a bit of sabotage here and there, a police station raided, a few R.A.F. airfields destroyed, nothing more than that. The English authorities know pretty well who's responsible, but they can't do anything about it. No Welsh witness would testify against them, and even if they did there'd be no convictions. Welsh juries and Welsh judges, you see. I say, I hope I'm not boring you with all this.'

'Just keep talking.'

'They're not strong numerically at the moment. They're in control of the Press and radio and education and local government and the Church, but their actual numbers are small so far. Though – I get all this from my brother-in-law, who's stationed there – it's true that they've grown a good bit in the last five years or so.'

'How's your brother-in-law making out?'

'Oh, quite well. They've no personal quarrel with the English, you see. He's not worried. There'll be plenty of time to get out before the shooting starts.'

'Now you're being fantastic. That's not the way they settle things in England.'

'This isn't England. The Welsh are Celts – like the Irish. They started shooting all right when the time came, remember?'

'What do they want, what are they after, these ... Welsh Nationalists?'

'An independent Welsh state. And they mean to get it. Of course, I've been exaggerating, really. No doubt you'd be perfectly safe in Lydney. I should say it's most unlikely there'd be any border raids or anything of that kind. Most unlikely.'

'These Nationalists. They Reds?'

'Some of them, probably. A bit of Communist backing, you know.'

The American drew in his breath sharply and sat for a few moments staring at the tips of his little pointed shoes. Bowen repented: he didn't want to spoil Lydney for him, nor in particular for his wife. He was on the point of urging the other to check up on the Welsh Nationalist story before making any kind of decision, when he squared his shoulders and faced Bowen.

'See here, young fellow. I don't know whether you've been trying to scare me, but if so you've been wasting your time. From now on I'm taking this Lydney idea a sight more seriously. And I'd like to say this. If any goddam Reds come snooping around my place, there's nothing I'd like better. No sir, there's ... nothing ... I'd ... like ... better. If there's any shooting, it'll be both ways. You can bet on that. I've always wanted a chance to get at those Commie bastards and this looks like it. Mm-hm. Well, thanks for the talk. It's been most interesting.' He banged his glass down, nodded once, and marched out.

Bowen felt less elated than he had a few minutes earlier, but he also felt a good deal tireder and drunker than when the American first appeared. Beddie-byes, then. The floor throbbed unpleasantly when he got to his feet, but he soon recollected he was on a boat, where engines were to be expected. With *This Rough Magic* under his arm he made his way downstairs.

Half-smothered in comics (a whole fresh supply had been bought in Southampton), his sons lay asleep in their bunks. His daughter lay asleep in her cot, holding a plastic bottle of purplish fluid at her side in the shoulder-arms position. His wife stirred as he went in. The movement put tension on some strands of hair and made her scowl fiercely without opening her eyes. Soon Bowen was aloft and lowering to the floor a series of objects that ended with all the life-jackets, stowed on his bunk for convenience.

Immediately he had put the light out Barbara said in her clear treble: 'What exactly was Bennie Hyman being so mysterious about this morning?'

In Bowen's mind alarm-bells began clanging, whistles blew, gun muzzles swung skywards, fighter pilots sprinted across the tarmac. 'Oh, it's just that they're keeping quiet about Strether's new book for the time being.'

'Ssshh, talk quietly ... Why?'

'Oh, they're not satisfied with it or something.'

'You didn't say anything to me about that.'

'Well, no, but I wasn't too sure of the position myself, dear.'

'Talk about it tomorrow. Thought you always told me everything.'

'But I do, I do. Honestly, dear. You know I do. Don't you?'

'You say you do, but how do I know whether you really do?'

'You must be able to tell I do, surely.'

'But how can I tell? What way have I got of telling?'

'Well, by knowing me. You know that's the sort of chap I am.'

'But I only know as much of you as you choose to let me know.'

'Now, fair play, dear, you know that isn't true.'

'How can I know?'

Bowen felt baffled. The next move in this ritual had long been laid down as the offering by him of caresses, at first

·repelled, then accepted, then returned; the move after that
··followed easily and naturally enough; and the move after
that was for him to go and make a cup of tea for them both,
which they would drink to the accompaniment of mutual
rallying, speculations about the landlord's amorous habits,
and the like. None of this was possible tonight. He wondered whether this point had just occurred to Barbara. He
said emphatically: 'Well, we can't really talk about it
now.'

'All right. Good night.'

He heard her thrashing about with pillow and bed-
clothes, plunging over from one side to the other, settling
down with a groan. Fix up about the coal bum, he thought
to himself, call in and tick the plumber off bum, see about
a new flat bum, ring up and put them all off bum, stop your
friends yelling and swearing when you let them out late at
night bum, really darling I think it's time we had a serious
talk *backside*. He wished he could meet himself, like Mau-
passant or whoever it was, but on a permanent basis. Then
he and the other chap could live happily ever after. Well, in
a way.

5

'Why isn't he here? Why isn't he here? Why isn't he here?'
Bowen asked hysterically some sixty hours later. He re-
ferred to C. J. C. Oates, the man who was going to put them
all up during their stay in Portugal and who was also,
according to his own account, going to have met them off
the ship. He had not done that. Bowen knew now that he
had known this all along, just as he had known that the
foreign A.A. chap – more precisely, the representative of

the *Automóvel Club de Portugal* – would not be present either. Well, it saved having to talk to him. On the other hand it meant having to talk to others. Although Bowen enjoyed chatting to his friends all right, and would even address strangers in shops, public transport and so on, he had never been keen on such involuntary chats as were involved in finding out official procedures, inquiring about the proper time and place for inquiring about things, and so on. He had no idea why this was, but thought it neurotic rather than ideological: perhaps he had been frightened as a child by a nasty manager of something. At any rate, he had never been able to book a room in a hotel without wishing he could produce a certificate of general probity signed by a doctor, a justice of the peace and a person in holy orders. Usually he tried, often successfully, to make other people act for him in all these matters. But that would not do today.

'Darling, do calm down,' Barbara said, grinning. She looked entrancingly neat in her white T-shirt with the thin horizontal navy stripes and her calf-length plum slacks, so much so that, given the chance, he would not only have performed the old marital rites but might have felt impelled to go on and eat her as well.

'Why did he say he was coming and then not come? Eh? Eh? Eh?'

'Now don't worry, he'll turn up.' She had apologized humbly to him on the morning after their how-do-I-know-I-know-you dialogue, and had been a very good girl ever since, carrying on nobly through her bouts of feeling seasick without any hint of self-consciousness. 'Look, there go the Marchants.'

These were a couple some years older than the Bowens, fond of talking and laughing, who they had met in the lounge on the second evening. Alec Marchant, a solicitor who practised somewhere in Essex, had endeared himself to Bowen by claiming a terrified ignorance of abroad. Bowen watched him now as he bustled round the taxi he had secured, hurrying the baggage-porter along, supervising the stowage of every item, gesturing freely and even apparently talking to the driver, getting in at last with a satisfied nod. Class traitor, Bowen snarled to himself at the sight. Imperialist lackey. Social chauvinist.

While he was listening to Barbara's reassurances, meditating on the deficiencies of his character and wondering what the Portuguese for 'I don't understand' was, the five Bowens were moving in loose formation towards the Customs shed: it could not be put off any longer. The first notable action they saw performed on foreign soil – apart from the thunderous anti-aircraft practice at Vigo the previous day – was a full-scale hawking-and-spitting demonstration by a handsome middle-aged man in an expensive suit. Both halves of the process went on for a long time and were very loud. David Bowen and Mark Bowen were fascinated; Sandra Bowen, who had fallen and grazed her knee, stopped crying. Garnet Bowen felt cheered enough to say to himself: 'My God, I'm abroad. Abroad. What about that, eh?'

All the Customs officers were distinguished-looking men who wore their grey alpaca uniforms with an air and yet with a hint of injured merit, like cashiered generals starting again at the bottom. The one Bowen got obviously felt his loss of status keenly, but between them they soon evolved an Anglo-Franco-Portuguese *patois* which, eked out with a bit of Latin on Bowen's side, served their purposes. Where was Oates, then? Bowen paid the baggage-porter, first ransacking the entire dock area for change. Bowen tipped the baggage-porter, giving him a number of *escudo* things that worked out, he supposed, at about three bob. The porter

54

swept off his hat and bowed. Bowen was to find out later
that this was not just Lusitanian courtesy (though it must
have been partly that), but a recognition of the fact that
one *escudo* (threepence) was the usual thing. Indeed –
Bowen was told later – it would have been ample, quite in
accordance with working-class wages; giving more would
help to spoil the market.

'Where's Oates, then?' Bowen asked his wife again, visualizing by now a mapless journey into the unknown. There
could not have been more than ten hours of daylight left.

'He can't have gone to the wrong ship, can he?'

'There must be very few ships called *Rio Grande* arriving
here this morning. He's forgotten. He never meant to come.
Are we sure this is Lisbon?'

'Cheer up, bogey, everything's going to be all right, I
know it is, I can feel it.'

Bowen said quickly: 'I wonder if that chap's him.'

'Ask him. He looks as if he's looking for someone.'

'No, you ask him. I'm tired of asking people things.'

Barbara threw back her head with a gentle yell. She was
sitting on the rail of a sort of cattle-pen arrangement inside
which, an hour and a half earlier, Bowen had talked to a lot
of different men about the car. Most of the time since then
she had spent trying to bend Sandra into an appropriate
position on her lap. She now made a gesture designed to call
this to Bowen's attention. 'No, you ask him,' she said.

Bowen asked him and had to admire the sincerity of his
regret at not being Oates. Then Bowen drove his sons away
from an inexplicable pile of straw they had started to dis-
tribute over the quay. 'Why don't you play with Sandra?'
he asked them.

'What at, Dad?'

From where he was standing he could see quite a lot of
Lisbon, if it was Lisbon. The buildings were a pleasant

colour in the strong sun, bright green trees showed among them, and the whole thing looked inviting and rather historical. It was a pity that so many non- and non-native speakers of English lived there.

He rejoined his wife, who was groaning a little to herself. 'Why don't you put her down?'

'She runs straight out of sight if I do. Why's it so hot?'

'Where's Oates, then?'

'Hadn't one of us better start asking about the place where he lives? He might be ill.'

'Look, I thought you were keen on the heat, and you haven't been in the place three hours before you start complaining.'

'He must be on the phone. See if you can give him a ring.'

'It's going to get a good bit hotter than this, you know. It's early yet.'

'Or that pal of Olivia's certainly would be. Can you remember his name? You wrote to him, didn't you?'

'I mean it's not only early in the day, it's comparatively early in the year.'

'What was it? Herries or Perries or something.'

'If you can't stand it when it's like this I warn you you're in for a tough time.'

'Ask this chap where there's a phone.'

'Dad.'

'Yes?'

'Isn't this Portugal, where we are?'

'So they tell me.'

'David says it isn't. And he keeps kicking me.'

'Tell him it is and kick him back.'

Turning away, Bowen saw Barbara in conversation with a couple of people. She grinned joyfully at him and nodded. The saturated solution of doubt, horror and despair that

56

had filled his veins was replaced in an instant by rich, oxygenated blood. Disembarkation bum was over – as if it had never been? But who could say what scars were left upon the spirit by such prolonged, grave nastinesses?

'Mr Oates? How good of you to come and meet us.'

'Not at all, Mr Bowen, I'm only sorry I'm late. These boats don't usually dock until about now, you see. May I present my wife? I hope you had a pleasant voyage?'

These and other amiabilities were uttered in a native English accent and with a not unattractive formality. Oates had a beaky, narrow face and hair shrivelling back from a freckled, deeply-lined forehead. Apart from a pair of large tan-and-white shoes, he looked in his neat dark grey suit like any young London office worker. His wife, olive-skinned and with other things about her that Bowen took to be typically Portuguese, seemed nice too. If she could have been compressed to about three-quarters of her actual width, she would have been very attractive.

The children were now introduced, Sandra from a distance because of having done what children of her age so often do. Oates, his comedian's shoes creaking like mad, led the Bowens away from the little area that, in their different ways, they had come to know so well. In the cobbled yard beyond the Customs sheds where the car was parked, he turned to Bowen. 'If you'll follow, Mr Bowen,' he said, 'I'll lead the way.' When this plan had been approved he moved off again with the slightly hostile purposefulness, like a hotel manager advancing on a drunken guest, that Bowen soon saw was habitual to him. Frowning to himself, he put on a pair of sunglasses and mounted a shiny, ginger-coloured, small-wheeled motor-bike. His wife got up behind him. Was he going to want him, Bowen, to do that too some time? (He was.)

Oates piloted them through the traffic – which moved

remarkably fast – with a hint of the exaggerated choreo-graphic swaying Bowen had seen gone in for by transatlantic dispatch-riders during the war. It was affecting to see how much he adored riding his bike. After a time they reached the coast road, the estuary of the Tagus on their left. Everything looked cheerful, expensive and brand-new, even vaguely important. Perhaps it was all to do with the sun and how bright it was. It was a pity that such terrible people said that colours were brighter in the South, because they were right. Oh well, they talked so much that they were bound to be right occasionally, just by accident. Bowen looked nervously about for peasants. It would be unendurable if they all turned out to be full of instinctive wisdom and natural good manners and unself-conscious grace and a deep, inarticulate understanding of death. But surely they couldn't, could they? No peasants were on hand to offer themselves as evidence. He had an uneasy feeling, though, that this state of affairs was not going to last.

'Oh, doesn't it all look lovely?' Barbara said.

It was no good. He had to admit it did. He felt suddenly almost mad with cheerfulness. He would be able to relax completely when the children were off his neck and at a distance and when he had satisfied himself that the accommodation was going to be all right. It ought to be, considering what they were paying for it: £185 for two months. It certainly seemed a lot, but then they had no idea of the market, and it covered full board for the five of them, and Seixas Peres, Olivia's in-laws' Lisbon pal, knew the Oateses personally. So it was going to be all right. Two bedrooms, own sitting-room, one maid living in, another maid by the day. Oh, smashing, boy. He was going to enjoy himself. He might even make a real, non-token start on that play. The only trouble was that he had so little to write about: the nefariousness of persons who made a living out of culture (but not enough of them were really nefarious enough), the difficulties of married life (but there were not enough of these, either, and he understood the whole idea very imperfectly), the momentous scope and variety of ways of being horrible worked out over the years by his mother-in-law (but imperfectly as he understood married life he could divine that that would not do. And the details of Mrs Knowles's behaviour were so finely discriminated that to change anything in the interests of camouflage would bring about a fatal dilution. Better just go on adding to his sequence of rhymes about her.)

At that point in his ruminations they reached an intersection where a traffic policeman stood on his little rostrum under an umbrella. He was another cashiered general, but wore a sun-helmet and was more than reconciled to his lot. Smiling, he blew his whistle at the converging stream and beckoned the Bowens on. Bowen cheered up again wonderfully and began planning the letters he would write on his return: 'Dear Dr Salazar, I feel I must write and thank you for the courtesy, the kindness, the hospitality ...'

6

'You've put her down now, have you?'

Barbara looked up from one of the women's magazines her mother had recently sent her. It was the kind that had pictures of rich people's houses in it, and Mrs Knowles's self-deprecation for reading such stuff would freeze the blood. She had the opposite effect on Bowen when she lauded the book reviews. Her daughter now answered his question: 'Yes, but I don't know how long she'll stay down. She hasn't finished her bottle yet.'

'Oh dear. How are her guts?'

'Only three times since this morning. Can I have a fag, sweet?'

'Sorry, I've only got Portuguese ones.'

'Never mind, I can't stand that brilliantine taste. I wish I could explain about Sandra's food to Rosie,' she said, meaning Oates's wife. 'The meat's always so rich. And why do they put olive oil in everything?'

'It's just a way they have. Did you try again?'

'Yes, only we're a bit stuck with anything more complicated than Yes and No. Why don't you try some French with her? Titus was saying she knows a bit of French.'

'I expect she does, but I'm not much good at Portuguese French. Ordinary French would be bad enough.' He sat down and picked up the postcard from old Buckmaster (or Strether) inviting them to call the following day. It would be a run of a dozen miles or so inland, he had worked out. He ran his eye over the card for the twentieth time, trying to solve the problem of what sort of man had written it, and also the rather more immediate problem of what that man had thought he meant by the map he had tried to draw on it. Revelation was withheld. Bowen went on: 'I hope those sores of Sandra's are going to be okay.'

'I've put some of that penicillin stuff on them.'

'Good for you. Where are the boys?'

'Off playing by the woods somewhere.'

Bowen made his way through a thin cloud of flies to the window. The sun, no longer intense, beat down on the splendid view of Estoril and Cascais with their palms and red roofs. Good stuff, Bowen thought. Even at this distance he could see the change in tone where the Tagus met the Atlantic. Running inland were the hills among which Sintra lay. The old wandering outlaw of his own dark mind had looked in there once, hadn't he? Bowen picked out the boys by their white shirts, trotting round and round each other in some gyration that was no doubt bung-full of meaning for them. He hoped they would not run across the fierce goat that had tried to butt one of them the day before. They were near the woods now where Oates sometimes took his gun of an evening to shoot at pigeons and what he called sparrows. (He hit them, too, as a recent lunch had acceptably testified.) One of these days it might be nice to accompany him. Looking nearer at hand, Bowen realized with some surprise that he had set eyes on an olive-grove. This might have had the effect of recalling one or two abroad-slogans, but this time what entered his head, for some reason, was that an olive-grove had been the scene of the surrender of Demosthenes's party towards the end of that unfortunate business in Sicily. When had that been? 415? 413? He had known once. Well, whenever it had been exactly, Sicily had been all right while Thucydides was on about it. That condition no longer held.

Bowen discontinued this and went on looking. A destroyer, doubtless part of the local navy, was standing out to sea. One or two canoes were still moving to and fro off the beach at Estoril, almost hidden by houses. Some fishing-boats were doing something in the approaches to Cascais harbour. He tried unsuccessfully to remember what Oates had explained to him about the way they auctioned the catch there. Oh yes, there was plenty to be got hold of in what he saw, if only one knew how. And if only, in addition, one could find some other jumping-off point than Titus Oates's house.

The minuteness of this house could still, after ten days, fill Bowen and Barbara with sincere amazement. The area of its ground (and only) floor could not have been much more than that of half a badminton court. In that space were assembled a lot of rooms. There was a dining-room with two large sideboards and a large table in it. Nearly all the pleasure Bowen had had since entering the house had taken place at that table, eating and drinking things that were on it. There, too, he had passed darker hours, working in the mornings at Barbara's instance on that awful play. His daily horror at what he had written the day before was topped up by the air-display put on by the flies that shared his occupancy. Roused to erethism by the heat, a pair of buzzing, copulating bodies fell every few minutes into his typewriter or hair – still, better that than into his soup or wine. He had had a wonderful half-hour with Oates a couple of evenings previously, syringeing the bastards; now and then Oates had let him borrow the squirter for a couple of goes. The flies had suffered frightful losses, but replacements had begun to move into the line within twelve hours.

The two senior Bowens shared a dark, wardrobe-ridden bedroom with their daughter. It had been ornament-ridden too until, ten minutes after their arrival, she had broken a richly-engraved scent-spray. The Oates's bedroom, piled with copies of *Tit-bits*, *Everybody's* and an old-fashioned-looking local effort with what could have been daguerreo-type illustrations, had turned out to be also the 'own sitting-room' the Bowens had been promised. They had actually sat in it on their first day. But now they were sitting, as they often did, on the beds in the boys' bedroom. Through a very thin wall was the kitchen. At the moment the two maids were cackling in it. Sometimes they quarrelled in it instead, or were denounced in it by Rosie Oates. They kept going on one or the other fourteen hours a day, while the baby of one of them sucked its dummy or slept, like an old man in the sun, with a cloth over its face. There was also the closet-like hall which doubled as the bed-chamber of the childless maid – so much for the opulent overtones of 'maid living in'. Last but very far from least, there was the bath-room-cum-lavatory. This it was the will of God that Bowen should now enter.

The rising graph of its smell seemed today to be reaching the steep part of the curve. Human effluxes formed the main theme, but there were decorative passages derived, less unmistakably, from decomposing talcum-powder, Oates's hair-oil, the gas from the monolithic geyser, exotic disinfectants, Oates's fly-squirter, damp towels and the for-midable orange-rubber enema-engine draped in glistening coils round the little cabinet. Wet sand from the children's feet gritted under Bowen's shoes. What air there was was hot. He wished the window had been made to open, he wished he could answer Oates's repeated reminder that they must say if they didn't like anything with a two-thousand-word (fifteen minutes' running time) harangue about the lavatory, he wished many things. Well, he told himself consolingly, it was no use expecting too much; after all, they were on holiday.

While making the stride that would take him back to the boys' bedroom, Bowen heard a childish wail through the clamour from the kitchen, where Rosie Oates was dealing out what he took to be denunciations and, it seemed, get-ting them back as well – with interest, as they say. 'She's awake,' Bowen said mournfully to his wife.

'Not surprising with all this row, I suppose. You know, I wonder how much longer we can stand it here.'

Barbara had begun wondering that on the fourth day and had been wondering it more and more often ever since. 'Do you want me to go this time?' Bowen asked quickly.

'Oh, would you be an angel?'

Sandra was standing up in her cot. Her face had a high polish and an expression of theatrical reproach. Placing it so that it looked over his shoulder, Bowen gave her *Ride*

a Cock-Horse in a light *mezza voce* baritone. He had a
theory that he could make it into a sleep-trigger by syste-
matic *diminuendo* and *rallentando*, gradually introducing
a slack, enfeebled intonation and so on. After fifty trips to
the door and back he had almost succeeded in getting himself off to sleep, but not his dear little daughter who, catch-
ing sight of him in the mirror of the most immense of the
wardrobes, gave a loud, hilarious snigger. He wondered how
long it had taken old Pavlov to get the salivation going
when he rang his bell.

Just then he heard Oates's motor-bike come popping
down the road and in at the gate, rev up mightily (as usual)
under the window where Sandra's cot was, then recede up
the path into the garage. The dog Blackie, a resident of the
chicken-run, flung himself to the end of his chain, barking
like a fool. The hens fluttered and protested. Oates called
some foreign matters to the gardener who came in for
an hour in the evenings. Why he came in Bowen never
quite discovered, for the two squares of barren reddish
clods that made up ninety per cent of this 'garden' – the
existence of which had been another selling-point of Oates's
in his letters to Bowen – never altered throughout their
stay.

Female cries of '*Bôa tarde, senhor*' – quite the old feudal
touch – greeted the master of the house on his three-yard
progress through the kitchen. Bowen could track him to his
bedroom by the furious creaking of his co-respondent's
shoes. He had never heard such a row. It was as if Oates had
a little amplifier-and-loudspeaker circuit wired up in each
heel. After a moment Bowen could hear Rosie come out of
the dining-room, her forty-minute task of laying the dinner-
table completed or suspended, and go in search of her
husband. Her sound was the shuffling clop of the loose fur-
trimmed slippers she wore. It was available at any hour of

the day and many of the night, and it managed to generate a really impressive charge of ennui. These two aural gaits, Bowen considered, had a good deal to say about the characters of their owners, like recurring sound-effects in some intellectual film.

Time passed. Oates arrived in the dining-room, turned the wireless on at something like concert-hall volume, and regaled the household with the strains of an American song about Spain being sung in German – a current favourite, this, on the Roman Catholic station in Lisbon patronized by him. The bawling and shrieking seemed to appease Sandra. Bowen laid her down and crept away.

More time passed. During this section of it the boys, having had their tea in the kitchen (egg and bacon for the tenth time in five days), were bathed and driven into bed. Here they began a long, bitter protest at having their parents sitting, so they alleged, on their feet. The wireless was now yelling what could have been a news bulletin. It all sounded as if it was very good news.

When Rosie appeared, did her shy, breathy smile and said 'Soup', the Bowen couple followed closely at her clopping heels. They greeted Oates, who smiled back with the air of inwardly suppressing the effect of some discreditable rumour about them he had picked up in Lisbon during the day. Then, frowning intently, he assembled what he would need immediately after the meal: his lighter, his packet of High-Life cigarettes (made from cigar tobacco or, more likely, cigar-butt tobacco), the coffee-machine with flask, trivet, burner, snuffer and bottle of spirit, the coffee-tin that had a picture of the Duke of Edinburgh's face on it, the special Coronation coffee-mug – most of these on a little table beneath a picture of Queen Elizabeth II's face. Rosie raised her soft moan, far different from her denunciation-screech: 'Lucia. *Sopa, faz favor.*' Now it only needed Oates to give an upward touch to the volume of the wireless, already relaying a girls' choir at a volume of a couple of bels, and the meal could begin.

It was an abundant and, to Bowen rather than Barbara, delicious meal. This was usual. Not before time Bowen experienced the onset of well-being. Soon afterwards they got his favourite radio commercial, of which the best bit was an announcer shouting with angry emphasis in a vibrated echo-chamber about a thing called Ideal Ginger Beer (and very good, in due time, Bowen found it to be). '*Ee-dee-owowowowowowl*,' the chap fumed, '*Jeenjer Bee-yeeyeeyeeyeeyeeyeer ... Casawawawawawa* Ee ... dee ... *owowowowowowl ... Alcantarawawawawawa* ...' Later they had *Three Coins in the Fountain*, a song – taken from an American film about some place in Italy — which handled abroad-sentiment on what Bowen considered to be a rather lower level, though much more succinctly, than the average travel-writer; it was a favourite of Oates's. They also had *A Pulha* or whatever it was; anyway Bowen had noticed it was a favourite of Rosie's and had gathered from Oates that it had something to do with a flea. Rosie laughed gaily at it. It's all right for you, Bowen thought to himself.

Oates took exception, as always, to his wife's enjoyment of *A Pulha*. He said it was the sort of song which only awful people liked. Awful people came into his world-view a good deal. They formed the bulk of the audience at Lisbon's cinemas, it was hard to avoid them when finding a spot for a picnic on a Sunday, they attended football matches, he encountered many of them on his shooting expeditions, they put money on the table at meal-times. He felt strongly on this last point, mainly but not solely for hygienic reasons. Bowen tried hard to imagine an awful person's lavatory. Oates now turned the wireless down, with a scowl that suggested indignant rebuke of whoever had turned it up. He said to Bowen in his gentle voice: 'Will you take some more wine?'

'Thank you very much.'

'You mustn't wait to be asked, you know. I hope you appreciate these Portuguese wines?'

'Yes, I like them a lot,' Bowen said, remembering in time that this 'appreciate' was one of the other's few straightforwardly non-English usages.

'Well, I certainly hope so.' Oates smiled diffidently and engagingly. 'You must forgive me for keeping on asking you whether you appreciate this or that. You see, I don't know you so well yet.'

'Of course, I quite understand. But you mustn't worry, really. Everything's fine.'

Bowen avoided his wife's eye as he said this. But, he asked himself, what could he say? To point out to Oates the deficiencies in his establishment would have meant deeply hurting his feelings, or demanding an intolerably radical change in domestic procedures, or – in the case of the overcrowding problem – exhorting him to run up an annexe, lean-to, etc., within the next twenty-four hours. Then, yielding top priority only to the lavatory question, there was the matter of Rosie and the children's food. The language difficulty was not so great as to have prevented her from understanding the Bowens' pleas for less fat-content, less seasoning, more variety and so on. It was just that, with the obstinacy of the really amorphous character, she knew better. Was it then to be suggested to Oates that he force her, if need be at the point of his gun, to go easy on the oil-can? Even this spectacle would not have relieved Bowen's feelings altogether; but then only *an hour of swearing* could do that. And he could hear Barbara's voice saying 'You'll just have to decide whose feelings are more important to

67

you, ours or the Oateses'' so distinctly in his mind's ear that he could hardly believe she had yet to say it in fact.

'Well, and how do you like Portugal?' Oates asked.

'Very much,' Bowen replied, adding silently 'for abroad', but otherwise sincerely enough.

'I hope you find enough in the way of amenities and everything?'

'Oh yes, it's all very good like that.'

'I'm glad you find it so. Of course, this isn't a rich country. That's what visitors so often forget. Though it's a good deal richer than it was before this chap Salazar came along.'

'Oh, he's, er ... improved things, has he?'

'Undoubtedly. You should see what he's done for Lisbon. The place has doubled in size since the war – yes, really. There's been a lot of slum clearance and so on. Now somebody like yourself coming from England, the Welfare State and everything, you might find plenty of things that would shock you. But that's not really the point. You've got to compare the place, you see, with what it was before.'

'And it was pretty bad, was it?'

'What? My God, it was terrible. Do you know – perhaps you won't believe this, but in the Thirties there were lepers walking the streets of Lisbon? I can swear to that because I saw one once when I was out with my nurse. Appalling. Only the rich people ever got any medical attention or went to hospital – well, there were no hospitals to speak of. All manner of epidemics running riot. There was a most frightful T.B. thing as well, and, er,' – he glanced over at Barbara – 'a lot of other unpleasant business too.'

'I see what you mean.'

'Yes. Well, this chap Salazar has got hospitals and clinics and convalescent homes going, and schools and orphanages – there's one just this side of Estoril on the coast road, you've probably seen it. All that sort of thing's expanding very quickly now. It's got to, by law. Salazar's seen to that.'

'Really?' Bowen rather liked what he had heard about Portuguese laws. One extra good one said that any restaurant meal that included meat must also include free wine. Another one said that you could eat one course at a restaurant and then validly plead hunger in your defence when the time came to reveal that you had no money. These were measures that no British Government could hope to get through, unless perhaps they were drafted to exclude from their provisions all poets, painters and sculptors, both supposed and real.

Oates was going on: 'And Salazar, he's a professor, perhaps you knew that, he manages to make the budget balance. Don't ask me how he does it, but he does. That was unheard-of, too. The fellows who were running the show before he came along just had no idea – getting the country into debt the whole time. The place had no sort of a future in those days. It has now. There's no doubt the Portuguese have every reason to be grateful to Salazar.'

When Oates was feeling his Englishness, as he clearly was tonight, his accent was as good as Bowen's (in fact rather better in some ways) and he talked about 'the Portuguese'. At such times he would compare the local navy disadvantageously, in point of size and quality, with the Royal one, disparage the country's music, point to the rudimentary stage its industry had reached, and be amused at such quirks as the recent decision that Lisbon, a compact city with no suburbs to speak of, should have an underground railway like any other capital. At other times he discarded the fact of his British birth and gave the Bowens a dose of his adopted nationality. This *alter ego* spoke English almost as idiomatically, but with what must have been a Portuguese accent, though it also carried a strong and perplexing

69

flavour of the Rhondda. Such was the sub-personality he adopted when he lectured Bowen, with abundant illustrations, on the post-war decline in the quality of British exports and in British business enterprise and reliability, or when he wanted to contrast British readiness to 'give away' India with the firmness that the Portuguese (who now became 'we') had shown over the Goa question. These and other opinions seemed dictated by his membership of Portugal's small, recent and – Bowen supposed – philistine and illiberal middle class. But the conflict in his mind, however partial and intermittent, between his Britishness and his Portugueseness made him more interesting to Bowen than that, and the neat symbols of that conflict, the souvenir-stall coffee-tin on the elegant traditional-pattern cloth Rosie had embroidered, seemed not only absurd.

'It makes me a bit fed-up,' Oates was going on, 'to think of all these attacks in the foreign Press by people who don't know the country. Salazar runs the place, admittedly, but it won't do to start comparing him with Franco. Franco's a real dictator – we know all about him in Portugal – he's very conceited, you know, having parades and things the whole time. Of course, the Spaniards quite like that, they're fond of ostentation and so on, always gone in for uniforms and flag-waving. From what I know of the Portuguese I'd say they wouldn't stand for that sort of nonsense – they're more like the British in that way. But in any case they don't have to put up with it, because there isn't any. In all the years I've been in Lisbon I haven't seen a single parade, apart from the Army, but that's different. And Salazar himself is pretty well a hermit, you know, lives very quietly. Yes, I support the régime all right, and so do my – well, my colleagues and friends.'

Barbara now startled her husband by asking a question. In company she tended to be silent, usually quite contentedly, sometimes – he thought this in his more querulous moments, when perhaps a policy statement from her had provoked him into a silent bum-recital – with the air of resting up until she could get him on his own again. She said to Oates: 'Is there a Labour party here?' By now they had reached the liqueur stage, and she was drinking *ginja*, a kind of high-octane cherry brandy.

Oates laughed with predictable tolerance. 'If you don't mind my saying so, that's the sort of question which only a person from England could ask.' He glanced at Bowen with raised eyebrows, perhaps to see if he minded him saying so; then looked at his guest's glass, which happened to be empty. Blinking thoughtfully, he got up and creaked sideways round the back of Barbara's chair to the smaller sideboard, along which were ranged the *cinzano*, the *ginja*, the two bottles of port, the *faísca*, the bottle of fruit extract for the children, and the *real fine eau de vie*. This last he picked up and, after making sure that Bowen wanted another drink and that this was the drink he wanted another of, poured him a respectable tot, managing well in the small polygonal space allowed him by the configuration of the furniture. 'You take this chap Gaitskell,' he said as he replaced the bottle – he never put it on the table unless de Sousa and Bachixa, his two motor-bike-owning friends, dropped in for a chat. 'Now you can't imagine him cutting people's throats, can you, or blowing up a bridge, taking money from a foreign power or anything like that?'

Bowen agreed, with some inward regret, that this would be wholly untypical. Out of the corner of his eye he saw Rosie take her translation of Hall Caine from the drink-sideboard and open it at a religious-looking bookmark.

'In other words he's a respectable character,' Oates was saying. 'Just as loyal to the Queen as anyone else. But the people who oppose the Government out here aren't like

71

that. Fortunately there aren't very many of them, and these Portuguese are pretty efficient at police work, so they don't get a chance to do much damage or kick up much of a row. But you take it from me. They're awful people.'

'I see,' the Bowens said simultaneously.

'Yes, when you really come to weigh it up, you know,' Oates said, lighting another High-Life, 'there just isn't any practicable alternative to this Government. Or any desirable one, either. It's got strong ties with the Church, which is as it should be in a country like this.'

His manner had lost its assurance and Bowen wondered whether he was going to bind them to silence and throw off the mask, reveal he was shortly booked to rush off on his ginger-coloured motor-bike and help to dynamite the casino at Estoril. But no: something in his immediate environment was troubling him. As he looked questingly about him it occurred to Bowen that perhaps it was the flies which were the matter – Bowen would be with him there, having had a courting couple fall into his *vinho branco* earlier. No again, which was a pity, for another drive with the squirter would have livened the evening up no end. His glance fell now on the wireless, which was quietly playing the slow movement of Haydn's 'Emperor' quartet; one of the great sane tunes of the world, as Bowen's programme-note expert (the doubt-horror-and-despair merchant) had no doubt felt bound to characterize it. Oates's frown, which had been comprehensive, became specific. He approached the instrument and with great stringency turned it off.

'This is pretty weird stuff,' he said.

7

Next day was Buckmaster day, and as full of splendidly straightforward sunshine as ever. At about eleven the Bowens piled into the car — all five of them, because although only one, or at most two, of them had any reason at all for wanting to see Buckmaster, there was nothing else to be done with the other three. Noting that Mrs Knowles's upholstery was already starting to age rapidly, Bowen felt at first a mechanical compunction, then a directed glee, for her last letter had contained a sentence enjoining her daughter to 'keep Garnett up to the mark'. This reminded him not only of the laughing moralistic vigour which she exuded at all contact, but of how her long-established misspelling of his name managed to taunt him with affected singularity, as if he kept insisting on spelling himself Robyn or Edmond or Donauld. Why was he too nice to point out her mistake *every time*, as she would have done in his shoes?

Sandra sat on Bowen's lap, though not at his suggestion. He soon began thinking about beer. He wanted a pint of English beer, but not because of its nationality or anything like that. Although Portuguese beer tasted much less of bone-handled knives than other continental beers, it still wasn't as nice as English beer. He thought of the time when Barbara, after a bad night with Sandra, had accused him at two hundred words a minute of pretending to like beer because he thought it was working-class, British, lower-middle-class, Welsh, anti-foreign, anti-upper-class, anti-London, anti-intellectual, British and proletarian. He had replied more slowly that she was mistaken if she thought he would deny himself large gins-and-tonic or magnums of sparkling red Burgundy just because nasty people liked them too. (How he thrilled to both the idea and the name of sparkling red Burgundy. Other entities had this same strange double appeal: rhythm and blues, dinotherium, deposit account. Little article there?) He had added to Barbara that beer was cheaper while still sharing with gin and Burgundy the property of making him drunk. This last factor had received insufficient acclaim. He thought to himself now that if ever he went into the brewing business his posters would have written across the top 'Bowen's Beer', and then underneath that in the middle a picture of Mrs Knowles drinking a lot of it and falling about, and then across the bottom in bold or salient lettering the words *Makes You Drunk*.

The car emerged from among some big trees with very green leaves into a declivity between some flowering shrubs on one side of the road and some squat bushes, arranged as if for ease of cultivation, on the other. Bowen liked seeing all this, and only wished he knew the names of the trees and the shrubs and the bushes, so that he could enjoy them more. Here and there were small houses, which he took to be the dwellings of the peasantry. Some members of this social group were almost continuously to be seen, working in the fields, strolling along the roadside or sitting round what he thought must be sort of well or pump arrangements. He inspected them as closely as he could for signs of instinctive wisdom and the rest of it, but all he could make out for certain was that they looked foreign, dowdy and on the whole rather amiable: some of them had even waved as they passed. He hoped they would stay amiable when he started asking them the way, as he would soon have to. They might turn grim then, a reaction which the obtruded contrast between their condition and his own would certainly justify.

When it came to the point, a signpost and a single mention of *a casa inglesa* (as rehearsed under Oates many times the previous evening) did the trick. Bowen felt quite the globe-trotter as Barbara turned the car aside on to an unmade track that curved away from the road. He proposed to regard the coming encounter as no more than exploratory, rather as it was regarded by Barbara, whom he had sold the idea that he was going to gather information which would help Bennie Hyman to launch a difficult book (this being a field in which she was mercifully vague), as well as, perhaps, getting material for a possible article of his own. A few years ago he would have felt a bit panicky at what was ahead of him, but now he didn't: those of his arrestingly varied and extensive shortcomings that failed to involve Barbara directly had come to appear to him as harmless quirks, even endearing little ways, like fear of cats or inability to mend a fuse. The most that he really felt was resignation at the prospect of being confronted by yet another practitioner of the arts. For Buckmaster was presumably the author of *One Word More* even if of nothing else.

The house, visible the next moment, seemed partly raised off the ground by wooden pillars. Everything was painted white, including a flight of steps with a handrail that had a creeper growing up it. A veranda looked as if it ran all the way round. Here a human figure stood, half hidden in strong shadow, apparently waving. It also apparently had a glass in its other hand. That was good.

While Barbara was halting the car in a small paved courtyard, Bowen was telling himself that he wasn't a spy, but a man doing a job. By the time he had leapt zestfully out of the car, burning his hand rather on some hot metal-work, and had turned to meet the man who was coming down the wooden steps, he was telling himself that he was a man doing a job and a spy too. Well, either way he might as well watch carefully.

'My name is Wulfstan Strether,' the man said, as at the start of one of those films where the hero does a running commentary as well as chatting to the other characters. 'And you, no doubt, are Garnet Bowen. And Mrs Bowen. And these are your children. I am very glad to welcome you all here.'

Bowen's first thought was Yes, claim upheld. Visually the fellow measured up : he was tall, slightly stooping, with almost white though abundant hair, and with a bearing, a nose, a mouth, a pair of eyes that could be unhesitatingly pigeon-holed as authoritative, hawk-like, sensitive, piercing. This was to ignore, perhaps, the properties of his ears (elongated, red), hat (staringly white), shirt (damask, extra-zonal, unwise), and his dialogue recalled Charles Morgan rather than anything Downing College would approve – though the distinction was admittedly a fine one. But all this was countered by the quality of his voice (the statutory reedy tenor) and its accent (older speakers' upper-class, with even a scintilla of *hyah* about the word *here*). He looked about sixty and, while amiable enough, a terrible old crap.

'Shall we go up?' he asked pleasantly. 'I think I can guess what bulks largest in your mind at the moment. A comfortable chair and a long cool drink. This heat, though not in any sense extreme, is, I know, or can be, not without a certain debilitative quality in its impact upon those unaccustomed to it.'

Barbara, carrying Sandra, dilated her eyes at Bowen and mounted the steps. Bowen, following with the boys, decided not to risk trying to warn them against saying, for example, 'Ergh, what's that?' in reference to their host, as they had recently said in reference to a fairly distinguished poet he had brought home for tea. He hoped it would not be as hard to avoid calling the old boy 'Buckmaster' as it was to avoid calling Oates 'Titus'.

They moved along the veranda. In some extraordinary way, Bowen found himself expecting some tall curvilinear beauty, golden-skinned and with blackbird-plumage hair (not to mention grace, pride, disdain – but with a hint of lurking voluptuousness – poise, etc.), to come forward and greet them. The woman who did had golden skin, yes, but it was old gold and accompanied by none of the other requisite attributes except disdain. She had that all right, and had it in the pure state, free from any voluptuary taint, thank God.

The room they entered was Maugham-like, but of the Far East and not the Riviera sub-type. Any whisky-sodden tea-planter or homicidal adulteress would have felt at home here in a moment, what with the venetian blinds, the hanging bowls with greenery trailing from them, the vaguely bogey-bogey wooden images (from Brazil, Bowen was told later), the magazines and novels from England – a promising field for investigation, these last. But was all that going to matter? Bowen felt now that within a few minutes, probably, Buckmaster would have produced some letter or other object which would establish his claim to being Strether. If it didn't come of its own accord, as it easily might, it shouldn't be hard to coax it out of him. Good. And drinks were on the way. Better. And, it suddenly occurred to him, no amount of spying could damage the old boy unless he was a phoney. Best.

The production of drinks was interrupted while Buckmaster went in search of ice. David and Mark had swept the room with a glance, found it void of entertainment material, and rushed out. Barbara had removed Sandra to less vulnerable ground. Bowen had the room to himself. He glanced along the bookshelves, which were of a pretty pinkish wood, unvarnished. A copy of The Custom of the Country early presented itself, but he set his teeth and went gamely on. *Under Western Eyes* bim bam a bomber bum. Then *Portrait of a Lady*. Oh, Christ. Uncontrollable laughter was the only dignified response to that. He vented some.

Buckmaster came back in the middle of it, naturally. Carrying an engraved silver bowl, he said that he saw that something was amusing Bowen.

'I don't know why, but seeing *Portrait of a Lady* on the shelf here reminded me of that time, you know, when old James made that comment on the shadow-play or whatever it was.' This remark sounded disagreeably knowledgeable to its author, who reassured himself by remembering that only a train-journey to Leicester (to hold forth on 'Crisis in the Modern Novel') and a shortage of reading-matter had led him on to the page of the *Sunday Times* where the shadow-play comment had been quoted.

'Oh yes. Yes indeed, one of the Master's choicest thrusts. "A remarkable economy of means *and of effect*," eh? *What?* HERM? *MM?*'

The surge of interrogatives was not unfamiliar to Bowen as a means, popular with elderly or academic persons, of underlining a jest, though it was a novelty to hear it used of another's jest. He smiled politely, thinking that a knowledge of Jamesiana, plus the possession of Jamesian texts, certainly befitted an indisputably major talent. Claim further upheld? No, for even a false Strether would be of this persuasion. A retired light-heavyweight, a devotee of Louis Armstrong or Pee Wee Russell would not aspire to be taken for a novelist of international repute. A pity, that, and a grave impoverishment of cultural life.

'Shall we venture on to the veranda, Mr Bowen? I think we shall find it cooler there. Is there anything you need, Mrs Bowen, for the, er, the *baby*?' Having successfully brought off this audacious colloquialism, he sat them all down and, tremulously and with excessive haste, poured

78

the drinks, rebuking himself under his breath for dropping an ice-cube, clashing two glasses together, serving Bowen before Barbara. 'It's a habit you pick up in these parts,' he said very loudly. 'Male primacy has never been lost, which, as a *mere male* myself, I am bound heartily to endorse.' He gave a gobbling laugh. Bowen and Barbara found themselves talking faster and faster about the weather.

After a time, the boys having chased each other away and Barbara having again removed Sandra from within range of breakables, Bowen said: 'Well, I should like to say how honoured I am to have come along here today and made your acquaintance.' He felt very horrible while saying this.

'You're most kind, Mr Bowen, most kind indeed. To one whose life as an artist is rounded, complete and now discarded, such kindness from one of your generation has the quality of a promise of support. I am grateful.'

'Then you're quite sure you won't write anything else?'

'Alas, yes. But why do I say alas? I have done what has been allowed to few men. I have performed what I was intended to perform and I have performed it well. It is my good fortune to be able to say with Mortimer that since there was no place to mount up higher, why should I grieve at my declining fall?'

'Well, yes, I can see that must be a comfort.'

'And since my lonely dedication is at an end, there is no reason any longer for me to prolong its circumstances. It is now my wish, for the years that I have left, to take that part in the life of my times to which my achievement entitles me. I plan to be in London at the time when my last work is given to the world, on purpose to study at close quarters the circumstances and effect of its launching, a form of self-indulgence which my creative regimen has hitherto denied me and which, I trust, may be deemed venial in one situated like myself.'

'Of course,' Bowen said vaguely, feeling rather over-whelmed. So Hyman, old Weinstein and the rest of them were going to have a lot less than a year's grace before Buckmaster arrived on their doorstep. Well, that was something pretty tangible to tell them.

'But it will be an impersonal study, for in a very real sense I am not concerned in it. Are we to call our former selves our own? By custom and courtesy only. In the fullest possible meaning of the phrase, I am not what I was. I have broken my staff, liberated my Ariel – a compelling image, it has always seemed to me, for the conscious resigning of the inspirational *daemon*. The moment I wrongly foresaw at the end of my penultimate work has finally arrived and passed. And so, on a more mundane level, I have had what I might perhaps describe as ... as a *spring clean*.' He looked squarely at Bowen with a sort of bland emphasis. 'Nothing remains to connect me with that former time. As soon as I had completed *One Word More* to my satisfaction, I destroyed all letters, all documents, everything inanimate, in a word, that connected me with yesterday. You will, it is true, find on my shelves copies of all my published works, alongside those of Jane Austen, of George Eliot, of Hardy, Conrad and James, of Stendhal, Flaubert and Proust, of the great Russians. But this is no more than one might expect to find in the library of any man who interests himself in observing the progress of the art of the novel. And such a man, at this time, am I. As perhaps you can understand, Mr Bowen, that little quirk of fancy provides me with vast amusement.' The amusement he then allowed to escape was not vast, but it was considerable.

Bowen went on talking somehow, trying feebly to extract some concrete reminiscence, some verifiable piece of information. But no: Buckmaster had never, apparently, met any living persons and few dead ones; none, at any rate, that Bowen thought to mention. The old chap had lived in Spain 'for some years' and had shifted to Portugal in 1936, having remained there 'for the most part' ever since. When Bowen tried to probe further he met with a reticence that could not be penetrated without seeming, or indeed being, vulgarly inquisitorial. It was almost a relief when Barbara returned and announced that they must be getting along.

Buckmaster became violently apologetic. 'But I have seen almost nothing of you, Mrs Bowen, nor of the charming youngsters. Will you not change your mind and stay to luncheon? Or at least permit yourself another drink? I am desolated. Well, we must arrange things more spaciously next time. I will insist on there being a next time, since I for one have immensely enjoyed today's occasion. And in my desire to talk about myself – for which I hope your good husband will pardon me – I have missed a rare, I should say an unique, opportunity for hearing at first hand how matters move in that strange world of London literary society. Well, it is only a pleasure deferred. On Friday I go to Coimbra for ten days or so, but on my return we must positively lose no time in renewing the acquaintance.'

'Are you visiting the University at Coimbra?' Bowen asked as they descended the steps.

'I may well do so, but my purpose is to be the guest of an old friend of mine who lives near by.' Suddenly twisting his head about like a frightened horse, he drew Bowen aside. 'Would you like to ... er ... *go* ... before your journey? And perhaps the children ... and ...?'

The lavatory was on the far side of the house at ground level. Its cleanliness made Bowen want to linger nostalgically there, but he repressed this. Idle curiosity made him go the other way round the building on his way back. This new route revealed to him a small garage, also built in under the veranda floor, with its door open and an aged car on view. Doing something to one of its headlamps was a young man who might have been a chauffeur. He was strikingly handsome and winked at Bowen as he went by. Oho, Bowen thought to himself. A far from whole-hearted devotion to the pursuit of girls had sometimes struck him as a kind of selection-board requirement for writers and artists. (Musicians showed up in a different light whenever they were sober enough.) This clearly had some sort of bearing on Buckmaster's claim, but just what particular sort was less clear.

Bowen and Barbara shook hands with the old boy. David and Mark did their stuff well and Mark added as an extra: 'What lovely drinks you gave us.' Sandra waved and produced one of her best grins. Buckmaster's face twitched about as he tried to conceal some of his delight. Bowen said as warmly as he knew: 'This really has been a great privilege, sir.' Saying it didn't make him feel terrible at all.

When they had driven away, Bowen's attempts to sort something out of the last hour's welter were interrupted by Barbara: 'That was jolly interesting, wasn't it? He was an absolute dear, didn't you think?'

'Yes, I did in a way, but he was pretty full of himself as well, you know.'

'Was he? He didn't strike me like that at all.'

'Well, you weren't there for that bit.'

'No, I know, I was minding the creature. Next time we really must see if we can't park her with Rosie and the maids. Still, I did see a bit of him. I'm going to enjoy telling Olivia all about it. See her eyes pop. He's a great hero of hers.'

Bowen winced. 'I'm afraid you won't be able to do that, dear.'

'Why ever not? Is there something secret going on?'

'Bennie Hyman doesn't want us to spread the word around at all until he says it's time.'

'Oh, damn and blast Bennie Hyman. What's it got to do with him?'

'Well, they are publishing this book of his, dear, old Buckmaster's, I mean old Strether's . . .'

'Look here, Garnet, there's something fishy going on, I know. I could tell from the way you and Bennie were muttering together the day we sailed. What's it all about?'

It always came to this in the end, and Bowen always thought at the start that it wouldn't. He told her the story, omitting only his hopes of a job with Hiscock & Weinstein and their contribution to his budget.

'What a revolting idea, spying on the old chap like that. Just the sort of thing I'd expect from Bennie. But I should have thought you'd have had a bit more integrity. I know you always laugh at me when I go on about integrity. Yes you do. But this time I'm right, and you know it. Don't you?'

'I suppose I do.'

'Well then. And what's the use of knowing what's right unless you act on it? You write to Bennie and tell him you can't help.'

'I can't anyway.'

'How do you mean?'

'Well, there just isn't any way of knowing about this business either way. Not from anything that'll come in my direction.'

'Never mind, you just contract out of it all. And I don't think you ought to go and see Strether again until you've made up your mind you are contracting out. Really, Garnet, how squalid.'

A lunatic shouting came from Bowen's stomach, the product of hunger mingled with fear. He hated opposition, not, he believed, because he liked his own way more than the next man, but because it made him feel so terrible, too terrible to sort out what he really thought. To decide whether, and if so how far, self-interest conflicted with decency over this issue meant using his conscience as a precision instrument. How could he do that with Barbara jogging his arm about integrity? Perhaps he'd feel better after lunch – roast sardines were promised for today – and a sleep. At least all this business meant he couldn't be expected to get on with his play for a bit.

8

After a morning's brain-pummelling about his conscience or his play (accompanied by fly-fighting), a hard afternoon on the beach (accompanied by wasp-evading and Sandra-chasing), and a dinner that featured a couple of pounds of pork a head, Bowen was often past his best when it got to half-past nine or so. But the advent, actual or predicted, of de Sousa and Bachixa was enough to drive him out of the room, which meant in practice (short of going to bed or curling up with a book in the lavatory) being driven out of the house. He had nothing against either de Sousa – the little grinning lemur-faced one – or Bachixa – the stout dignified good-looking one. But de Sousa spoke almost no English and Bachixa, though he spoke some, obviously spoke far more Portuguese. The Bowens were therefore reduced either to sitting there while Portuguese was talked, or to making de Sousa and Bachixa sit there while English was talked.

It was this situation, rather than any hope of getting in touch with local life, which took the Bowens out one evening soon after the Buckmaster lunch. They were bound for the café in Estoril, a seaside resort which Bowen considered could lay a very fair claim to being dubbed the Blackpool of the South but for its smallness and lack of amenities. They avoided the casino, the only other evening attraction, reasoning that they could light their cigarettes with a 1,000-*escudo* note any time they felt like it and have the rest of the evening to themselves. At least that was how they put it to each other. What they liked was sitting in the arcade of the café drinking excellent local gin-and-tonic at not much over half the English price, plus the equally excellent local liqueurs at ninepence the large tot. It would be very easy, cheap and pleasant, Bowen often reflected, to drink oneself to death in Portugal. Perhaps he would try it some time.

As they swung down the dusty lanes, passed the barracks with its ill-clad sentry and moved towards the coast road, Bowen was meditating. Fleas were the object of his contemplation. He considered them an integral part of abroad, so much so that their occasional presence in the United Kingdom might well be the result of successive importations from the Continent. Perhaps it was a flea of Latin origin that had made half a term at Swansea memorable for him. He was in digs at the time, where the presence of four ginger cats, one of them called Ginger, had already tried him a little. The reign of the flea began when he was just about coming through on the other side of a thirty-six-hour stomach-ache. He was also attending a course of lectures on some piece of orang-utan's toilet-requisite from the dawn of England's literary heritage – *The Dream of the Rood*, perhaps, or *The Fall of the Angels*. He felt it would only take one more visit from the dough-faced Christian physicist who lived upstairs, or one sight of a soccer forward-line embracing one another after the scoring of a goal, to send

85

. . . him straight into whatever international brigade might be available at the time. Instead, he got the flea.

There was the bathing, the changes of clothes, the dosing of his bed with the Atomic Insect Destroyer ('They Are *Paralyzed* – Then D I E') which turned the sheets into hot sandpaper. The flea stayed alive and biting. He lay nude in bed with the light on and a wet cake of soap in his hand. Nothing happened. He knew now that fleas, like colds, acne and lumbago, belong to a part of the natural order where there are no cures and the only thing to do is to wait for them to go away. This flea fed and roamed freely for weeks; then, after keeping himself to himself rather longer than usual, he crawled down on to his host's wrist while the latter was drinking a Guinness in the upstairs bar of the Bryn-y-Mor. Bowen blew at him and he vanished. He never saw or heard of him again.

When the fleas began in Portugal Bowen felt, as one who finds Mont Blanc impressive or sees a knife drawn in a Shanghai bar, that tradition was reasserting itself. He should also perhaps have taken warning from Oates's revelation that, before he and Rosie came along, their house had been occupied by awful people; but what could he have done? Anyway, the Bowens counter-attacked fiercely : lots of baths and bathes for all five, frequent and diligent inspection of the kids, he and Barbara dashing into their bedroom several times a day to strip, as if assailed by intolerable lust. They gained ground slowly and unsurely; it all contrasted interestingly with the war of movement on the fly front. Bowen's first kill was a big insect with an important, matriarchal appearance. About that time, acting on the principle that suffering is the raw material of art, he began devising a flea episode (later rejected) for his play. A man called Bellow was going to catch the flea that had been devoting its attentions to him and somehow convey it to the person of the villain. After a couple of happy days spent watching his enemy scratching and cursing, Bellow was destined to pass an amorous afternoon with his young lady. That night, finding the flea back in residence, he was to spend in scratching and gloomy speculation. Thereafter invention along this line had failed.

If Bowen had acquired his Portuguese fleas in the course of roughing it, being put up by a brigand in a cave, dossing down on straw in a tavern yard, that kind of thing, he considered that he would have felt differently about them. They would have become a troublesome but distinctive token of manhood, like sabre-cuts or venereal disease. That was how some of his friends seemed to regard fleas and other 'little inconveniences' you found abroad. But as things were the fleas had come to him, not he to them. He had just been quietly minding his own business. Shame as from a boil on the neck, nostalgia for the neat little South Ken. bathroom, decreased tolerance for Oates's creak and Rosie's clop – ever in his heart, these.

They reached the café. Barbara had stopped mentioning Strether and integrity in the same sentence and only chaffed him now about the business. She was looking fine this evening, trim and brown and larger of eye than ever. Bowen rather wished she wasn't: the wakefulness of Sandra in the same room, the readiness of the springs of their bed to click and twang at the slightest movement, had been restricting their married life a good deal.

Soon after their first drinks arrived a man who said he was called Gomes came over to their table. 'Do excuse me for intruding,' were his first words, 'but I heard you mention things about London and I couldn't resist coming and talking to you. Tell me, what's the old place like these these days? I haven't been there since before the war.'

By this time he was sitting down, offering cigarettes and

87

signalling for another drink all round. It very soon emerged that he had been educated at Oxford; either that or he had taken some trouble to be able to impersonate one who had. His face and – apart from his cream shirt and lavender tie – his dress were of clerical sobriety, but his demeanour was not. He had a brilliant mirthless smile with clenched teeth and a trick of nibbling the inside of his lower lip. Bowen could guess his age (fiftyish) and his income-level (highish). He told them nothing about himself beyond his name and the fact of his English education.

They moved off London after Bowen had tried to tell him what the old place was like these days. Gomes said: 'It doesn't sound like my London. But isn't that rather true of Britain as a whole – do forgive me if I sound offensive; it's just that I'm concerned at what I read of these post-war changes. This Socialism, now. Are those fellows going to get back into power again, do you think?'

'I hope so.'

'Oh, do you? Then you're a Socialist? Do pardon my curiosity.'

'Well, in a way. I certainly prefer them to the other crowd.'

'The Conservatives, the Tories? Really? I'm astonished to find a person of your obvious high education opposing the Tories. You mustn't mistake my meaning – I'm merely saying that it's a revelation to me. Perhaps I'd better explain that I value the ideals of English Conservatism highly; I used to think they were just English ideals in general, but I'm talking now of thirty years ago, you understand. I knew some fellows at Balliol – I was next door myself, at Trinity – they used to say I was a sort of incarnation of Conservatism, much more perfect than any Englishman could be. They said they could promise me a safe seat if I cared to stand.' He gave his sudden grinning smile. 'But you

88

don't want to listen to my autobiography. No, what really attracted me was the terrific emphasis on freedom you get. That's my quarrel with your Socialists, they don't really believe in freedom, do they?'

This was just Bowen's question. Like an examinee who has been lucky with the papers he proceeded to give Gomes a totally false idea of his political knowledge. Gomes listened carefully, biting the inside of his priestly face, not breaking in when Bowen ordered more drinks. Gomes was drinking Scotch, the most expensive drink in Portugal and therefore, Bowen was told on another occasion, obligatory among well-off people whatever their digestions felt about it.

'Well, this is most reassuring,' Gomes said when at last Bowen fell silent. 'I certainly had no idea the people in your Labour Party were taking these problems so seriously. As you say, I've probably been reading too much Tory propaganda.' He grinned again, then went serious. 'It's marvellous to think of all this kind of thing being discussed openly, in Parliament and the Press, quite freely, no censorship or anything like that.'

'The censorship here's pretty fierce, is it?' Bowen asked.

Gomes reacted like a man in sudden pain, clenching his jaws and drawing in his breath. As if he found it hard to get the words out, he said: 'If it won't bore you, let me tell you something of this wonderful country where I have the honour to be a citizen. Yes, the censorship is, as you express it, pretty fierce. All publications of any kind have to be passed by the censor. I don't mean just newspapers and such things, though I may say that includes periodicals to do with football, you know, and the home and so on – they're all examined for something the régime doesn't like. Why, you can have no idea of what this entails. If you want to get up a charity or something like that, something utterly harmless, then you must first get the authorities' permission, and if you have a printed prospectus, then that goes to the censor automatically. If you so much as hold a dinner and send out printed invitations, you must let the censor see those too. And what the censor doesn't like – well, it's something that suggests something is wrong somewhere; it doesn't matter what or where. I'm not talking about actual complaints against the Government: you go to prison for that. Do you know who trained our secret police, that fine body of men? The late lamented Himmler, with personal supervision. But this censorship: for instance, there's never any word of public health in the papers, except the pious statements that it's marvellous, couldn't be better – with the worst slums in Western Europe right on our doorsteps in Lisbon. You can't even say things are improving; that suggests they aren't perfect. Again, accidents. They're just never reported. It might shake the public confidence. I'll give you an example: you see this railway here?'

Bowen said he did; it ran along the coast from Lisbon to Cascais and, though posher and faster, had often reminded him of the tram-like train running between Swansea (Rutland Street) and Mumbles Pier: the oldest passenger railway in the British Isles, too.

'Well now – do say if I'm boring you, won't you? – part of the embankment thing collapsed one fine day and the train ran smack into it. A small baby was killed and a woman died in hospital. Several people badly hurt. Now then. Only one paper printed this news, by an oversight I imagine. Our brave policemen came along and closed it down for a month as a warning. A warning not to depart again from the official policy to cheat and to lie.' He said this rather good-humouredly over his shoulder as he waved and hissed for the waiter. 'Then of course all the film posters are censored. In the interests of public morality, naturally. Have a look next time and you'll see the stamp. It's the Church behind that. Don't please misunderstand me: I'm a serious Catholic myself, or so I should like to think. But I can't forgive the way the bishops are with Salazar in everything. And the priests. There are plenty of good ones, naturally. But for many of them, you see, to be a priest is an escape from poverty – some money in your pocket at last. No feelings of religion at all. Two friends of mine, good Catholics, started a little soup-kitchen in their village up near Braga : free soup twice a day and bread for the children of the poor. The priest preached against them from his pulpit; it was the blow to his prestige. Actually the Church is pretty unpopular in some areas, especially among the poor. Down south recently they were rebuilding a church that had been burnt down. Well, the local poor decided they had done very well without the Father preaching there, so they all got drunk one night and pulled the place apart again. That sort of thing would make you smile, perhaps. It makes me feel sad.'

Saying this in a noticeably buoyant tone, as before, he ordered drinks from the waiter and, it soon transpired, coffee and cakes as well. Bowen took the chance of moving his eyebrows and head in such a way as to ask his wife if she wanted to leave. She didn't. When Gomes had finished his negotiations, she said :

'Someone was telling us the other day that Salazar has done a lot for the country. Do you think there's anything in that?'

'Well, my dear, the hospital situation is less of a crying scandal now, yes. A few clinics for syphilis, just here and there. But it's all window-dressing really. Our fine feathered friend Salazar must keep well in with England and America now, since they didn't become defeated by Hitler as he'd hoped. He wants money from the democracies, you see, so

Lisbon, at any rate, must be brushed up a little, there must be some evidence of welfare. It's paid him well in all sorts of ways. That fine new road, now, running east from Lisbon to Evora and Spain – that's an American road. It'll take up the supplies to the N A T O armies in Spain when they try to stop the Russians at the Pyrenees.'

Bowen gave a light, devil-may-care laugh under his breath at this prospect, then ran a finger round under his collar. It stayed hot late in Estoril.

'He gets money inside Portugal easily enough,' Gomes was going on, glancing without affection at a group of rich adolescents, all white shorts, T-shirts and red jockey caps, who were fooling about round a British-made sports car at the kerb. 'Anything he wants, from a church to a cruiser, he just blackmails the big firms : if you won't buy it for me, then no more Government contracts for you, my fine fellow. Money is the key in Portugal. Or the spending of money. In England or America, if a man makes a good pile he goes on working, making more, and continuing to give employment, which is a thing your Socialist friends leave out of account, if I may say so. Here he just spends it with as much fuss as possible, piling his wife and his lady friend with diamonds and furs and so on, and making spoiled brats of his children – like that crowd of imbeciles there.' One of the T-shirt bunch, a pretty, nasty boy of about fourteen, was displaying the abandoned, single-minded ferocity of a toddler as he demanded something from a smaller replica of himself. 'In England, it's from the sons of the rich men that you draw so many of your splendid public servants, your officials in the colonies, your administrators, and your novelists and poets too. But these – they think of nothing but cars and new clothes and entertaining themselves. They're like women. Here in Portugal we have conscription, as you have in England. But these bright lads will never join the Army; their pappas will see to that, bribe some fashionable doctor to give a medical certificate that they're unfit. You imagine if that was tried in England. Your Queen herself joined your women's Army. You imagine the row which would be kicked up if some rich Englishman tried to keep his son from conscription. No, my dear fellow. The rich men of a country, if they have the sense of responsibility, can be everybody's salvation. Without that responsibility they bring shame and ruin. Have a cigarette.'

The parts of his discourse were too neatly dovetailed not to make Bowen suspect that it had been delivered, in substance at least, many times before. It was easy to sympathize with him. Beyond talking like this to strangers he could have few outlets, given a muzzled Press, the presence of Himmler's graduates and the absence of political parties. Bowen could not visualize him tying himself up with Oates's awful people for a spot of bridge-demolition, but he had met hardly anyone whom it was easier to visualize blowing up a bridge if it came to the push and given the right company.

Gomes lit their cigarettes with an apparently gold lighter the size of a pocket dictionary. 'It may interest you to know,' he said vivaciously, 'that I'm now engaged in breaking the law.'

'By talking to us like this?'

'That too, yes. If you were a journalist I should get a stiff sentence. But I hardly think that the discretion of English people leaves me anything to fear. However, I was referring to the lighting of your cigarettes. That's illegal, you see. Oh yes. I can pass you my lighter and permit you to light your cigarette with it. Or I can light a scrap of paper with my lighter and light your cigarette with the flame of the paper. But I mustn't do what I've just done if I want to remain on the right side of the law. This is incredible to you, but it's a fact. It nearly baffles me. It's connected with the efforts of Salazar to make it difficult for the owners of lighters. The makers of matches complained that their trade was going downhill, because of so many lighters, and Salazar had to pacify them for his own ends without offending the lighter people too much. So the owner of every lighter must have a licence, for which he must pay, and there are all these other rules.'

'It sounds fantastic.'

'Yes. But this country is full of such fantastic things. A few years ago there was a new law which made it compulsory for every bathroom and lavatory to contain a *bidet*. I think Salazar must have had a friend who made the things. He must have known that the facilities were inadequate for most of them to be connected up with running water, not enough skilled labour and so on. So he just made no reference in his law to connecting them up. And now all over Portugal there are thousands of *bidets* in the lavatories, all standing in splendid isolation.'

'So that's it.' The Bowens exchanged grimaces. One mystery (but not the most urgent) about the fittings of Oates's lavatory was solved. Perhaps if they hung on long enough they would pick up a hint or two on how Oates got hot water from the geyser to the washbasin, in order to shave there, in the absence of any hose or visible container. At that time Bowen was coming round to the view that Oates must carry on his person some kind of collapsible jug.

Gomes had fallen silent. His face hung down in a depressed way while he nibbled its interior; then it brightened with what might have been triumph at the sight of the pretty, nasty boy bawling tearfully as he pursued, with an out-of-condition, slacker's gait, his retreating companions. Bowen felt his own face giving itself over to a spiteful grin.

94

After a moment Gomes said: 'I'm afraid I've been letting myself go. Do forgive me for talking so endlessly. It's a great fault of mine, I know.' The Bowens' protestations failed to stem a prolonged flood of eloquent and documented self-deprecation. He defended himself tentatively by suggesting that it was good for English people to hear what he had to say. Far outdoing him in vigour, the Bowens aided this defence. He got up in the middle of it, put some money on the table and said abruptly: 'I hope you'll enjoy your stay in Portugal. For the tourist there are many attractions; for the resident, not quite so many.' He softened this rather cinematic apophthegm with a cordial handshake and a warmer version of his smile. His final wave, delivered from the driving-seat of one of the most unnecessarily large of all the unnecessarily large cars on view, was also cordial.

As Gomes drove violently away he seemed to be leaving behind him the impression that his audience had failed him in some way. Not having had a couple of armoured divisions (with sea and air support) to place at Gomes's disposal, Bowen could not see how this could have been avoided in large part. Still, a penumbra of trivial insularity had been pretty effectively cast over British domestic squabbles about housing policy or the next round of wage claims. This endemic drabness would no doubt be dissipated, Bowen reckoned, if Tories could actually be witnessed in the course of jubilation over something or other to do with capital gains, if Labour could arrange to televise a *bona fide* very fat man occupied in watering the workers' beer. But as things were, Gomes seemed to have provided yet another excuse for people like Bowen to be politically apathetic at home.

Bowen himself was beginning to wonder if apathy might not be defended by pointing out that too little of it could bring a nation (France) to the edge of chaos, when his wife said: 'Well, that was jolly good copy for you, anyway.'

'Yes. Don't know whether I can use it, though.'

'Whyever not? You could alter everything about him so that Salazar and his friends would never know it was him.'

'Yes, but you could never be sure it wouldn't put them on to him. I shouldn't like taking that sort of risk.'

'And yet you were quite ready to spy on poor old Strether. You are funny. I shall never work you out.'

'The two things are completely different, dear.'

'You think they are. Because talking to Gomes or whatever his name was was like something out of *Good-bye to Berlin* and the Strether business is just to do with a lousy old writer that people have got no business to be reading anyway. According to you.'

Bowen raised his eyebrows. 'There may be something in that.'

'Well, if there is, don't just say so and go on as you were before. You're getting much too good at doing that.'

9

Bowen was thinking what a dreadful thing the theatre was as, a couple of mornings later, he unshipped his typewriter on Oates's dining-table. His 'rough draft', now unavailingly headed 'Final first draft', had got to page 19 again, the point where twice before he had ripped it up. The present version differed from the earlier ones chiefly in the number of transparent patches, formed by the cream Barbara used to alleviate flea bites, which mottled its surface. He put a fresh sheet in and, after spending a few moments wishing he were doing something quite different, typed:

GREGORY: But this is really quite farcical.

Like all the other lines of dialogue he had so far evolved, it struck him as not only in need of instant replacement, but as requiring a longish paragraph of negative stage direction in the faint hope of getting it said ordinarily, and not ordinarily in inverted commas, either. Experimentally he typed:

(Say this without raising your chin or opening your eyes wide or tilting your face or putting on that look of vague affront you use when you think you are 'underlining the emergence of a new balance of forces in the scheme of the action' like the producer told you or letting your mind focus more than you can help on sentences like 'Mr Recktham managed to breathe some life into the wooden and conventional part of Gregory' or putting any more expression into it than as if you were reading aloud something you thought was pretty boring (and not as if you were doing an imitation of someone on a stage reading aloud something he thought was pretty boring, either) or hesitating before or after 'quite' or saying 'fusskle' instead of 'farcical'.)

Breathing heavily, Bowen now x-ed out his original line of dialogue and typed:

GREGORY: You're just pulling my leg.

Then he got up and stumped round the room for a bit, clawing like a science-fiction monster at the flies which wove about him their delicate flight-patterns.

All right, why was he writing this thing? Partly because he could not simultaneously join in the forenoon watch of wasp-evading and Sandra-chasing on the beach, nor was there any danger of enforced participation in a game of ball in Portuguese. Further, shameful as it might be to admit it, the idea of the play had started to interest him rather. It was called *Teach Him a Lesson*, and was about a nasty man (the Gregory whose disavowal of credulity he was currently toiling to refine) and the nasty practical joke played on him by his nasty friends with nasty consequences. The friends were supposed to be less basically nasty than Gregory, but somehow got infected by the very nastiness they were setting themselves to avenge. Like nearly all Bowen's artistic impulses, this derived from a long voluptuous daydream about getting Mrs Knowles expelled from civilized society. Unfortunately the idea had lost some of its urgency in being modified, in obedience to the reputed rule that none but aesthetic considerations must dictate the shaping of a work of art. Having his way with Mrs Knowles on paper was becoming an obsession with him and provided the sole possible reason for getting divorced from Barbara. Even with no holds barred he would probably only be able to get one book out of Mrs Knowles, but Christ, what a book it would be. A gorgeous, star-shot, blood-red, awesome pall of hatred.

His mind groped painfully back to the theatre, that vast battlefield of taxi-getting, being on time, cloakrooms, programmes, waiting, tipping, no cigarettes I'm sorry sir, other entrance sir, two lagers four and six please sir, you can't put your coat there sir, well Ken my dear just simply went overboard about it, but my dear you just have to admit it isn't an Anglo-Saxon thing I mean look at O'Casey, look at Dylan, and if you aren't terribly careful my dear you'll have me shouting Wilde and Nolly Goldsmith and Farquhar. Why was it that everybody who had anything to do with the theatre went on as if they had everything to do with the theatre? Why didn't master printers and binders and the girl who worked the switchboard at Hiscock & Weinstein go on about Evelyn and Graham and Tony and Nigel?

And go on about them *all the time*? And go on about them *in such a way as to stop anyone in earshot from going on about anything else*?

Bowen made another line of x's and typed:

GREGORY: Don't give me that.

After that he felt he had given the creative process enough outlet for one morning. The trouble was that he was committed to providing further outlets on succeeding mornings. His only hope lay in establishing some real foundation to his vague suspicion that someone had used his *Teach Him a Lesson* idea before. Well, you couldn't force that sort of thing. It had to come of its own accord.

He next picked up and re-read the mysterious letter from his landlord that had arrived, thanks to miracles on the part of the Portuguese postal authorities, the previous day. After a salutation that featured one of the less common allotropes of Bowen's surname, it said that the writer had been thinking things over again – in itself a questionable claim by one so clearly unused even to once-and-for-all cogitation. If Bowen considered himself entitled under the agreement to the room on the half-landing, it was further stated, he should confirm same at once with a view to matters being regularized. After that all there was was 'Yours Knowland'.

Had the landlord really been ennobled during the last couple of weeks? No; he could not have been. What was 'same' that Bowen was being asked to confirm at once? Was he really to write back saying Yes, he did consider himself entitled to the room on the half-landing? The letter was a very appropriate sort of document to receive abroad, in that it used the English language to suggest a rich variety of possible meaning, like a revolutionary kind of poetic style. Bowen was reminded of the forms he had had to fill in in order to get the car on board the *Rio Grande* with them. One extra good one had had spaces headed '*Reg. No.*', '*Serial No.*' and '*No.*' on it, and he had had some marvellous fun reeling round the flat swearing about that one; but the best of the lot had had '*Type*' on it in two different places. Which of them meant which of the answers 'Morris', 'Morris Minor', 'Saloon', 'Private Car' or (since the form said it could be used for motor-bikes as well) 'Car'? In the end he had just said 'Type' to himself and written down in both cases what first came into his head, as if taking part in one of those tests where words like 'love' or 'lavatory' are used as response-detonators. He had thought at the time that to fill in the spaces with something like 'oxymoron' and 'valve-trombone', say, would have done just as well, and that the only real purpose of the form was to remind you that doing something you didn't want to do (like going abroad) was going to be just as hard as doing something you did want to do. More and more his life was becoming a matter of grimly going on day after day trying to persuade his mother-in-law to spend Easter with them – symbolically, anyway. By Christ, and actually too, by Christ.

These thoughts depressed him, and in addition brought no nearer a settlement with Viscount Knowland. After some time he was persuaded that the air of mystery here arose from drink or dementia rather than anything so practical as chicanery. He put himself on record to the effect that he did indeed consider himself entitled under the agreement to the room on the half-landing.

Short of devising a yet more succinct expression of Gregory's scepticism (too depressing) or going down to the village for a quick one at the wine-shop (too likely to be menaced by staring children, footpads, etc.) there was nothing to do until lunch-time. Of course, he could always have a nice read. Try this, now.

It was with a sense of having by now earned the right to attempt penetration of the hard confident sheen that had, since the first morning of his stay, overlaid in her grey-green eyes the smoky tumult he had glimpsed there that spring evening (the strange light all velvet and honey) – it was with such a sense that, presented now with her vigilant yet dreamy profile (it wasn't much good wasting time at *this* stage on speculations about the significance of that comma-shaped mole on the nostril-wing) as they stood at the open-flung window – before which in the flinty afternoon sun a bougainvillaea waved – Frescobaldi brought to utterance : 'Do you come here often?'

'What a strange question,' lightly.

Well, he was not to be put off. 'You're waiting –' he teased.

She was facing him now. The faintest flicker, too slight to be called a tremor (what, nervousness in *her* regard!), came, went and came again in the dear pallor of her cheek, as if some small fish-shadow had flicked away into a pool's darkness at a dreadful strange heavy tread – *his* tread? But there had not been, he'd thought, that in their talk, even earlier, which would of a sudden have brought this to her. 'For nobody' – it was quick, level-spoken, and in anyone else, anyone less careful, he sensed, always to appear to match a mood, would perchance have seemed to scout him – 'that you know.'

He reached towards her with 'How can you be so sure?' and the moment he had awaited, his words barely out, came. With an almost audible snap the bright shell of light that hid her eye-depths was, in but an instant, gone and vanished, and the tumultuous whirl beneath was his to gaze and guess at. Tumultuous? – why, certainly! – and yet, through all those maddening smoke-bedevilled galleries of ambiguity there rose up – to meet him, *him*? or was he a mere tourist of others' feelings, for whom the cataract would leap, the geyser spout, the dark waters still hold mirrored a speaking artifice of lighted towers as indifferently as if none were by? – there rose up in Yelisaveta's eyes, at all events, the unmistakable intimation of a power that was also a consciousness of power, a still certainty far remote, indeed, from the turbid middle depths of the grey-green orbs and nearly as far removed, in some octaves of its implication, from the almost insolently shallow self-confidence of their surface which even now, as he prolonged – with something not at all distantly akin to terror – his gaze, silently re-formed, as the first touch of winter would breathe upon some rush-fringed pool a coating of ice thinner than gold-leaf, inexorable in its very delicacy.

A protest, then. He tried 'You'll know me again', but this spun wanly away down the gulf between them, a poor scrap of anonymous pasteboard let fall from a night-lit window. More firmly: 'What is it that, my dear, would seem to be, now, the matter?' – and on the instant before his eyes there wheeled momentarily, duskily, the vision of black sea-flowers at a depth coiling offendedly aside at the lurching, slowed fall of a rotting and timbered prow, won from deck and keel by soft century-long motions at the sea's floor. No earthly power would have stopped him, now, from turning away.

But she followed him, her hand lighting upon his arm. She had understood. She, somehow, had seen it too.

You go out of your way to tell us how, Bowen inwardly recommended, as once to Frank Sinatra in the long-ago. He wanted to put the man who had written that in the stocks and stand in front of him with a peck, or better a bushel, of ripe tomatoes and throw one at him for each time he failed to justify any phrase in the Frescobaldi-Yelisaveta scene on grounds of clarity, common sense, emotional decency and general morality. Alternatively he could turn an honest dollar by getting in first with something he might provisionally entitle 'Full Fathom Five: an examination of light and water imagery in the later work of Wulfstan Strether'. Yes. Was there really a Prospero tie-up here? If so it might be significant, for what he had been reading was One Word More. A *conscious* attempt to echo This Rough Magic on such a level might well occur to a Cambridge, Mass. sophomore with his head stuffed full of Blackmur and Burke, but hardly to an oldster like Buckmaster, who probably thought *The Sacred Wood* a bit new-fangled and clever-clever. On the other hand, an *unconscious* Prospero thing in *One Word More* did seem to go some tiny way towards suggesting that its author was also the author of *This Rough Magic*. Unless, sod it, it merely pointed to the devotion with which Buckmaster had soused himself in Strether's work. And was there really a Prospero tie-up anyway? Bowen felt that he would never be sure now.

Feeling that he would never be sure now about almost any given problem was beginning to obsess Bowen to a degree comparable with the liquidation of Mrs Knowles. For instance, his uncertainty about whether or not it was right to spy on old Buckmaster now felt more or less permanently jelled. (Jelly, while he was on imagery, was a pretty good equivalent for the properties of his mind, Bowen decided: it was soft, it set easily, and it shook whenever anyone went near it.) Anyway, he now felt convinced, or felt he thought he felt convinced, that Buckmaster must be Strether. It was so unlikely that he wasn't. On the other hand – and why was there always another hand? and not just *a*nother hand, but half a dozen? – *Briareus and Scaevola: an examination of the predicament of modern man*, by Garnet Bowen: Hiscock & Weinstein, 25s. ON THE OTHER HAND, that earthquake they had had along the road a couple of hundred years ago must have seemed almost inconceivably unlikely right up to the time when the first tiles started dropping. Mm. You never could tell.

The sound of the Morris coming up the road reminded him of his wife's existence. Right: whatever the rights and wrongs of the thing, Barbara must not be allowed to prevent him from doing what he felt he wanted to do, such as it was, about Buckmaster. There was a sound from his stomach as of convivial, Friar-Tuck laughter: it knew lunch was imminent. He went to the window. The boys, full of fun, were conducting a running fight with each other as they got out of the car. They at least were having a whale of a time abroad; perhaps in years to come they would thank their old father for having, at untold cost to himself, taken them to foreign climes before their attitude to these could be vitiated as his had been. Then came Barbara, carrying a yelling and stiff-backed Sandra.

Bowen's heart went out towards his wife. Poor little thing, he thought, this is a pretty poor sort of abroad-holiday for you, and you were so excited about coming. She looked at the same time fit and haggard; her eyes, brighter and clearer even than usual, were rolling a little in weary protest. All right, Oates, this is your lot, Bowen said to himself: smarten your bloody ideas up or . . . Or what? Well, or something, anyway; you wait and see.

10

'Come,' Bachixa said politely. 'You will see my bicycle now. It stands just over here, sir, by the gate. It's an English machine, you know. In Portugal we think they're very good. They have good power, also when they're older.'

It was with a sense almost of anticipation that Bowen followed Bachixa's stocky lumberjacketed figure down Oates's minute drive. He was already by way of being an authority on Bachixa's motor-bike, both as regards its recent and its more remote history. He knew all about the soft-rubber handgrips and their advantages in a hot climate, the devoted watch on fuel consumption, the slight but recurring trouble with the chain, the tellingly long life of the tyres. There was also the envy manifested by the owner's colleagues at the Lisbon shipping office where he worked, though this was hinted rather than itemized. Never to cast eyes on this bike would have seemed to Bowen a readily endurable deprivation, but Fate was not to be turned aside.

They reached the bike. It was rather smaller and less florid than Bowen had expected: no twin fins or vast fluted cylinder. In fact it looked just the thing for a rural dean's crazed widow to go and buy the cat's-meat on, especially in view of its crimson velveteen saddle-cover. It clearly inhabited a more spacious and sedate world than either Oates's ginger-coloured German model or the Italian motor-scooter favoured, as Bowen well knew, by de Sousa. (Where was he, by the way? He and Bachixa were so much a dual phenomenon that to see only one of them carried intimations of sudden illness or arrest.)

Wincing softly through pursed lips, Bachixa sprang smartly forward and dusted the speedometer-glass with his cuff, then leapt back to a stand-at-ease position at Bowen's side. Together they ran their eyes over Bachixa's possession, the latter in quiet pride, Bowen in quiet search of material for comment. The silence lengthened and he could feel Bachixa starting to eye him. Without looking (he hoped) too much like a man in an advertisement being given an electric shaver by his girl, he tried to filter on to his face an expression of gratified desire. 'Well,' he said unguardedly, 'she certainly looks in tip-top shape.'

'She ... ?'

'I mean everything is in very good condition.'

Bachixa shrugged his shoulders, as if to say 'What else?'

'Er ... the paint's new, isn't it?'

This time he smiled eagerly. 'Ah no, sir. In last December. It was the best paint. And ...' Quickly and dexterously he threw open the tool-case and shook out a spotless sky-blue duster. 'I clean with this all the painted parts, every day. It's the best idea.' He flicked off-handedly at the front mudguard.

'I agree,' Bowen said warmly. 'You burn a mixture of petrol and oil, I think you said?'

'A mixture, yes.' The duster refolded and restored, he threw his leg across the saddle and settled himself comfortably in the riding position. The seconds went on ticking by while he went on sitting there and Bowen watched him. So did the policeman's two children across the way. Bachixa glanced loftily at them. Don't mind me, Bowen wanted to say to him: go *brrrmmm, brrrmmm* if you want to. But why should he want to? He rode the thing practically all the time, didn't he? Then whence this symbolical re-enactment?

When Bowen was wondering whether to tiptoe away, Bachixa dismounted with a sigh, smoothed out the wrinkles in the saddle-cover and adjusted the waistband of his lumberjacket at the regulation level. 'You would like, sir?' he said.

'I would like?'

'You would like to try?'

'Oh, well, thank you very much, yes.' Bowen got on. Try? Try what? How did he mean, try? He sat there trying for some time, his brain slogging about for a peg on which to hang superlatives. In the end he said emotionally: 'Very comfortable.' He jogged up and down a little. 'Most comfortable. And everything' – he gestured towards the exhaust-lifter, the handbrake, the ignition-advancer-and-retarder – 'so . . . nice and handy.'

Bachixa digested this, nodding to himself once or twice. Then he said: 'Would you like to take a ride, sir?'

'That's very kind of you, but I don't think I could manage the gears and things.' Bowen laughed ingenuously. 'It's been so long since . . .' He could easily remember his last motor-bike ride. It had been on an old and massive Army machine which had unseated him at 10 m.p.h. and then tried to roll on him.

'I will drive, of course. You may sit behind me.'

'Well, actually, I don't think I've got time, thanks all the same. My wife and I are going . . .' In a pig's ear I may sit behind you, Bowen thought to himself. Oates hadn't got him on to a pillion yet and he was damned if he was going to let Bachixa work the trick.

'It will take only five minutes. And I drive very safely.'

'Oh, it isn't that . . . Ah, here's your friend.'

Bowen was overjoyed to see and hear de Sousa rounding the bend on his pale-green motor-scooter and coming to join up with Bachixa, thus restoring the order of things as well as providing a felicitous diversion. As he approached he was already smiling more broadly than many people can manage; when he dismounted he began laughing. In him these two responses had little intermediate ground. Bowing deeply to Bowen, he cackled out 'Good evening' in English, then put his bike on its rest, came over and shook hands. As soon as his eye fell on Bachixa's machine, his demeanour sobered, became scrutinizing, even censorious. Pointing at something, he rapped out an expostulatory question. Bachixa retorted vehemently. De Sousa scowled and his voice rose.

They were hard at it when Barbara appeared, all tizzied up for the evening and looking faintly delinquent as a result. De Sousa at once began laughing again. They both said 'Good evening' as they shook hands, but Bachixa added 'madam' to it.

'Bôa tarde,' Barbara said, blushing slightly.

'Ah, bôa tarde,' de Sousa chuckled to Bachixa, in case he

had missed this stroke, then, again bowing, he said it back to Barbara. So did Bachixa. He had started laughing too, perhaps at the fact that de Sousa was doing so much of it, more likely by simple infection. Both of them were dancing about a little. They reminded Bowen of the two students from what was then the Gold Coast whom he had once seen snowballing each other outside one of the Swansea lecture-rooms.

Bowen was soon shaking hands again, first with Bachixa's substantial cushiony one, then with de Sousa's delicate gibbon-like one. They both said good-bye, but Bachixa added, not smiling much, that he would drive Bowen another evening. As the car moved off Bowen could see the pair of them returning to the charge by Bachixa's bike. He wished more than ever that he could speak Portuguese.

The reason for the uniquely early appearance of de Sousa and Bachixa at Oates's was that they were to have dinner there, a revel made possible by the Bowens' invitation to dinner at the Pensão Internacional in Estoril. Their hosts were to be Alec and Edith Marchant, the couple from Essex whom the Bowens had met on the *Rio Grande*. They had exchanged addresses before parting, but a link-up had seemed unlikely until a precarious telephone-call, marked by much repetition of '*Como?*', '*Que?*' and less identifiable particles by operators and other intermediaries, had taken both parties to the Lisbon fair.

The Bowen party had included the Oateses, de Sousa and Bachixa. The last-mentioned had explained that the fair, which ran right through the summer months, was 'in favour of the poor', and Bowen had felt that he himself was, too: he had seen some Lisbon poor by then. In the course of the evening he was first gravely unmanned by a go on the water-splash, which involved an unbanked right-angle turn at about 100 f.p.s. in a small open car affair – and then

108

railroaded into throwing down spiced-beef hot dogs, cream cakes and sparkling, or rather fuming, vin rosé. Just as his stomach seemed on the point of spontaneous combustion, he had heard Alec Marchant yelling his name from the immense tractor-drawn, balloon-tyred limber in which sightseers were towed round the place. Since this equipage could be neither halted nor boarded, Bowen-Marchant contact had been momentary, partial. Barbara had pointed out the existence of the loudspeaker system to a Bowen who felt like a non-rigid lighter-than-air craft; Rosie had taken him across to headquarters. There, eager to practise her English, she had knocked a text together while he belched like a seal. Soon a voice was bawling and rebawling: 'Will Mr and Mrs Ma-russian . . . please go to the fez office . . . big-house Mr Bone . . . is wetting for dame.' It had been quite a short wet.

Outside the Pensão Internacional the Bowens speculated briefly about the other people they were to hold themselves in readiness for meeting that evening. There were the Bannions, who were resident in Portugal and had evidently taken the Marchants under their wing; and there were the Parrys, figures of distinctly minor importance who would not attend the meal and might even, it was envisaged, not appear at all. Bowen wondered to what extent the Parrys' arrival on the scene, if it did indeed take place, was designed by Alec Marchant to slake an imagined thirst on the part of Welsh people for one another's society. Such a design showed consideration, which was far from negligible, but also a pardonable ignorance of what Bowen had often thought of patenting as Shenkin's Law. This said that Welshman A encountering Welshman B outside Wales will find that Welshman B is exactly the sort of Welshman that Welshman A left Wales in order to avoid encountering. How did Englishmen get on? He must ask one.

He turned these matters over in his mind while Barbara and he took photographs of each other (result: B.B. – French teenage novelist; G.B. – King George VI enjoying joke; remarks: neither destined for Mrs Knowles's album. Disposed of as follows: B.B. – negative and print secreted in G.B.'s desk drawer; G.B. – negative and print torn up small and thrown into R. Tagus). Then they went in.

Alec and Edith Marchant were waiting for them in the garden and introduced them to Isabella Bannion, a smiling bespectacled Goanese lady in a splendid scarlet-and-green sari. The impression she made was of inextinguishable good-nature. 'So nice,' she cried, seizing both Bowens in turn; 'aha, so nice, so nice. Tell me, are you having a nice holiday, a really really really nice holiday? That's right. Harry is coming soon, he'll be down soon, in just a minute. You must sit down, sit here, yes, you here, Mrs Bowen, and you over there, Mr Bowen. That's right. Have a cigarette – no no no no no, have one of mine, you must try them, put those away, Mr Bowen, please. Alec has a match. You like brandy and soda? You both like brandy and soda? Aha, that's good. We find it best to have it out here like this on the tray, the bottle and the glasses and the soda, we call it soda but it's really the natural-gas mineral water they bottle here locally and I'm sure you'll find it very good – and the ice here in this pretty bowl. Isn't this a pretty cloth, Mrs Bowen? It's the local style of embroidery, you know, all done by hand, of course. Every Portuguese girl learns to do this work as part of her education, just like learning to cook and keep house. Ah good, Alec, you're a very quick barman, I shall be able to recommend you if you ever want to change your job. There we are, we all have what we want. You talk to Alec now, Mr Bowen. Edith was telling me about your children, Mrs Bowen. You have three? So young to have threee children, so young.'

Holding a gigantic brandy-and-locally-bottled-natural-gas-mineral-water, Bowen did as he had been bidden while Isabella Bannion's husky, compelling voice ran on in the background. Alec Marchant filled in a few details about the Bannions, who were friends of a friend of his and who, immediately upon meeting him and Edith for the first time, had begun showing them Portugal without any regard for trouble or expense. All four had recently returned from an expedition to Fatima, where the religious festival had been on. The Marchants had personally witnessed a great number of processions, all of them strikingly elaborate, and had attended several full-scale services, two of them at night. Isabella Bannion had taken it upon herself to see that they missed nothing of interest or importance, and had been far more informative than any guide-book could have been on the provenance and significance of all that they saw.

'Well, you certainly made the best possible use of your time,' Brown said.

'Oh yes, we weren't idle for a moment. We owe the whole thing to Isabella.'

'It seems to have made a profound impression on you.'

'It's not the kind of experience you forget in a hurry.'

'I can believe that. I suppose you've finished seeing the sights for a bit now?'

'Oh no, there's a lot of stuff in and around Lisbon we've still got to see. This afternoon we all went to Belem. Have you been to Belem?'

'No. What happens there?'

Marchant drained his glass and refilled it. 'Well, there's nothing that actually happens, if you know what I mean. You go and look at the tower, you see. It's a very nice tower. It was put up in the early sixteenth century, or was it the early fifteenth century? One or the other, I'm pretty sure. Isabella explained it all to me. And then when you've

. . finished looking at the tower you go and look at the monastery. I shouldn't have wanted to miss that. Then tomorrow
there's the Palacio Foz and the art galleries. Or are we going
to Sintra to look at the palace there? Either way we're
getting our money's worth all right. Have another of these,
won't you?'

Marchant went on to say that Isabella Bannion was very
devout. She had done a great deal of work for her Church
in Goa and had received a personal commendation from
Salazar. It appeared that in Armacão, the little town on the
south coast of Portugal where they lived, she had continued
her activities with the help of her husband. They had
adopted as their son a young priest who already occupied
an important position in the local hierarchy. From all that
he had heard and seen, Marchant had concluded that religion played a large part in the Bannions' lives.

'You mean they're always doing good works,' Bowen
said.

'It's far more than that. You see it most with Isabella.
She prays a lot.'

'Always popping in and out of churches, that kind of
thing?'

'That's hardly the way to put it. And it isn't only that.
She prays wherever she may happen to be, on the beach, in
the car, having dinner and so on. Harry joins in.'

'What do you and Edith do while they're praying? Do
you join in as well?'

'No, we're not expected to. We just keep quiet. She does
it so naturally it's not in the least embarrassing. You'll see.'

'How long do they last, these prayers?'

'Never more than about a minute. Sometimes there's a
hymn after it's over. Edith and I often join in that.'

'I shouldn't have thought you'd know many Catholic
hymns.'

'Oh, they aren't Catholic hymns. Harry isn't from the South, you know; he was a Belfast Presbyterian before he was converted. He knows a lot of Moody and Sankey.'

Bowen nodded. 'The good old good ones,' he said.

'Isabella has a direct personal relationship with the Virgin, actually. She takes care never to ask for anything unless it's really important and not for herself alone. And the funny thing is that her prayers are always answered. I said I didn't believe it at first, but she quoted so many instances that I just had to give in. Can I top that up for you?'

Marchant spoke next of Harry Bannion. He had met his wife in India, where he had held a senior post in a foreign bank. He had also been high up in, perhaps even at the very top of, the Indian Boy Scout Movement. On retirement, his wife's connexions with Portugal and the thought of the ravages which British income-tax would inflict on his pension had combined to settle their choice of domicile. Marchant said that Harry Bannion was something of a character, or 'card', while sharing his wife's kindness and generosity.

Just then a tall, large-featured man appeared at the top of the short flight of steps that led to the nook where they were sitting. His face had an expression of elaborately assumed severity. When everyone had seen him he snapped to attention. 'Come on now,' he shouted, 'smarten it up a bit. Out all cigarettes, pipes and Woodbines. Look lively, there. Wipe that grin off your face, Marchant. Company . . . *shun*. Stand-at . . . ease. Stand . . . easy. But beware, beware, because' – he broke into exaggerated *bel canto* – 'the Sergeant-Major's on parade. Yes, the Sergeant-Major's on parade.' Rounding this section off with a brief tap-dance, he approached and peered frowningly first into Barbara's face, then into Bowen's. Next, he backed away and struck a considering posture, head cocked, hand splayed over chin, elbow on palm. 'Now don't tell me, let me guess,' he said. 'Let's see . . . Now this' – he jabbed a finger at Bowen – 'must be ... Mrs Bowen ... and this' – jabbing at Barbara – 'by a process of elimination ... must be Mr Bowen. What? What's that you say? All right, you needn't shout, I'm not deaf, just a wee bit hard of hearing, like. Well, speak up, you needn't darn well whisper. What? I've made a mistake? I have? Impossible. Well-nigh unthinkable. The last of the Bannions in error? Never let it be said ... But if so be that the sense of the meeting hath run against a Bannion, then it behoveth and befitteth the said Bannion that he ack-knowl-edg-eth his aforementioned error, and God save the king. A million pardons to you then, madarm, and to you likewise, monsewer. Lo, I have spoke. Oogh! Hot, isn't it? Ah, well done, thou good and faithful servant.' This was to Alec Marchant, who as best he might had been mixing him a drink.

'I should think you could do with one after that turn, Harry,' Marchant said.

'Well now, me boy, and to be sure it's meself who wouldn't be argying with ye there, bedad, and that's the truth of it now, so help me. Here's mud in your eye, all.'

'Ah, Harry dear, you must give time for Mr and Mrs Bowen to get used to you, you know,' Isabella Bannion said indulgently. 'He's always acting these parts of his to make people laugh,' she explained to them.

'Well, when you stop smiling you start dying, that's the way I look at it,' her husband said, winking at both Bowens in turn. 'Now tell me, what do you think of Portugal? It's your first visit, isn't it? I'd be very interested to hear how the old place strikes you.'

They talked vaguely of this – at least Bowen was a bit vague – till it was time to eat. By then he was beginning to feel drunk. He had discovered that the Bannions, although moderate themselves, liked you to drink up and also liked refilling your glass before you had laid it down after drinking up. Marchant was later to put forward the claim that he himself had been drunk twice a day ever since meeting the Bannions.

Their entry into the dining-room caused a notable stir among the twenty-odd persons eating there. Some smiled and nudged one another; some displayed nervous expectancy; all were affected in some way. Bannion addressed them all from the doorway: 'Senhoras, senhoritas, senhores, members of the First Gilwell Troop, I salute you, one and all. To each of those here present I award the Silver Wolf, and to all your heirs and assigns of appropriate age goes a Bushman's Thong. Be of good cheer, lift up your hearts, for the hour of deliverance is at hand. Naught shall make us rue, if England to herself do rest but true. This programme comes to you by courtesy of the makers of Bannion's Brobdingnagian Brandy Balls, Inc.' While the rest of the party were taking their seats, Bannion went over to two middle-aged ladies who were sitting nearby. 'Bon soir, mesdames,' Bowen heard him say. 'La plume de ma tante est dans la poche du jardinier, ah oui oui oui, zut alors, bon voyage, n'est-ce pas?' After some more in the same strain, which was received with bewildered amiability, Bannion approached a handsome dark man who was by himself eating lobster. 'Buenas noches, amigo,' he said, taking a claw from the man's plate and cracking it. 'How's the old battlecock and shuttledore? Bless my soul, but this is uncommonly good provender, what?'

'Who's that chap?' Bowen asked Marchant.

'Who, that chap? Oh, he's the ex-tennis coach to the king of Portugal. Spanish chap.'

'But there isn't a king of Portugal, is there?'

'Isn't there? Well, perhaps he's tennis coach to the ex-king of Portugal, then. I know ex came into it somewhere. I could have sworn.'

'But wouldn't the ex-king of Portugal be a bit past tennis by this time? I seem to remember he was chucked out in about 1908.'

'In that case it must be the son of the ex-king of Portugal. Either that or this chap's the son of the ex-tennis coach. What about some wine? Will you have the *branco* or the *tinto*? I can recommend the *tinto*. I think they make it from blackberries instead of grapes.'

'Sounds delicious.'

While Marchant poured him half a pint or so of dark red wine from a huge wicker-covered jar, Bowen watched Bannion seemingly imitating a frog to the dynastic tennis coach. The latter's head was thrown back in rich, urbane laughter. There was a lot to be said for Bannion's method of dealing with the abroad-problem. Flaunting national differences dissolved inhibition far more efficiently than trying to ignore them. And only an unusually nasty man could have resented Bannion's approaches.

After the meal Bowen walked carefully with the others into the lounge, which exuded a sparse but clean Victorianism. Here Bannion greeted presumable Americans and Scots with cries of 'Howdy' and 'Hoots' before seeing about coffee, liqueurs and cigars. Without being aware of it having started, Bowen found French being talked to him by a middle-aged lady who might have been one of the ones Bannion had told about his aunt's pen, but who might not. The French went on for a time he could not measure. He made little of it beyond an occasional word like *le* or *je*, but it was clearly of a narrative or expository character. Bowen unbuttoned his shirt and scratched a small chaplet of flea-bites on his chest. Why was he standing up when the first armchairs he had seen since getting off the boat were only a few feet away? He went on putting this query to himself until the French left off. Then he went across the room to where a cup of coffee and two glasses of *conhaque* were waiting for him. He drank them all. The brandy, he noticed, was not Oates's *real fine eau de vie* sort, but the ferocious-port sort. He went up to the lavatory.

It was very fine up there: all the usual fittings, including a *bidet* in evident working order, no dirt of any kind any-where, and a faint, cleanly smell. He found he was breath-ing as if he had just run a race. This seemed important to him, but in some way he could not define. He sensed the almost-completed departure of his grasp of detail, and in-deed of broad, approximate issues as well. The thought of Strether, totally absent for several days, came to him. He remembered fairly clearly having written to Bennie Hyman explaining the position. That action was about as remote to him now as the onset of puberty. He must think it over again. Oh, God, how could he? Glancing up he saw that the lavatory, or its cistern, was entitled 'The Energetic'. Barbara would have known how to interpret that omen.

11

Getting unquestioningly into Mrs Knowles's car (with no more apparent interval than if it had been parked outside the lavatory) Bowen burnt both hand and lip on a cigar he was smoking. He sat and watched its smouldering end fall somewhere among the many pairs of feet that covered the floor. He was still turning this over in his mind when all the people started getting out again. It was dark, but there were plenty of lights to be seen, especially round an area where a lot of men and women – and children too, he noticed –

were sitting at small tables. Around him there was a general movement in that direction. He joined it. On the way he passed between a pale-green motor-scooter and a smallish motor-bike with a crimson velveteen saddle-cover. Near by he made out a ginger-coloured machine that somehow suggested Germany to him. The sight of them surprised him less than he felt it should have done.

Edith Marchant said: 'How are you feeling, Garnet? . . . Oh.'

Isabella Bannion called out: 'Harry, Mr Bowen would like a glass of mineral water. A big big big one. With ice. And then lots and lots of black coffee. Quickly.'

Dear Mr Nehru, Bowen thought to himself: hands off Goa. If Goa loses her identity, it will be the end of something unique, something noble and wise. – In another mood, he knew, generous tears would now be coursing down his cheeks.

Time passed while he drank various fluids. Then, as he lifted his head, a scene sprang into view with all the briskness of a television programme coming back on the air after a breakdown. He was at the café in Estoril with his wife and friends around him. He was moved. 'Welcome home,' Alec Marchant said.

A small boy touting lottery tickets approached Harry Bannion. 'Not tonight, Josephine,' he countered, then twisted in his chair and flung up a hand: 'Amigo. Hoy. Amigo. Yes, you. Wake up there. Come and have a drink. Your last chance to take advantage of our great free offer. Pull up a chair. Dress off to the left, now, you women.'

The tennis coach, smiling with conscious but readily forgivable handsomeness, was drawn into the circle and very quickly handed a whisky. Harry Bannion at once rose to his feet and rapped on the table with a coffee-spoon.

'Ladies and gentlemen,' he said hectoringly, 'a little reci-

tation entitled *The Charge of the Light Brigade*, by William
Makepeace Longfellow.'

'This is a good one,' Edith Marchant whispered to Bowen.
'We had this at Fatima.'

'... First as recited by our friend the Vicar.

   'Hawf a league, dearly beloved brethren, hawf a league,
     Hawf a league, oh bless my soul, onward,
   All in the valley of the shadow of death
     Rode the blessed six hundred.
   "Forward in the name of Jesus ..."'

'Harry,' Isabella Bannion said in smiling reproach.

'All right, my dear, dinna fash yourself.

   'Forward in the name of Jesus, the Light Brigade!
   Chawge for the guns of hell!' he said:
   Into the valley ....'

'What's this, a variety show?' a voice asked at Bowen's
side.

It was Oates in his best suit and grinning. Behind him
were visible Rosie, de Sousa and Bachixa, sitting at a table
a few yards away. They all waved in their various modes.
There was too much noise for de Sousa to be audible, but it
was plain from the movements of his head and body that he
was laughing.

The restoration to Bowen's brain of something like normal service in sound and vision had yet to reach the higher
centres of that brain. 'Come on, Charlie,' he said vigorously,
using for the first time the name Oates had asked to be
called by. 'Bring 'em over. Bring 'em over. Bring 'em all
over. We'll have a drink. All have a drink.'

   'Arf a league, arf a bloomin league,
     Arf a bloomin' league honward,
   HaÎl hin the valley (wotcher cock) er death

Rode the six undred, eh, mite?
"Swelp me bob, forward the Light Briggide!
Cor lovaduck, charge for them blinkin guns ..." '

All the people Bowen had ever met in Portugal seemed
to be assembling round the table. It would not have surprised him at all to spot Gomes's sacerdotal figure, hardly
at all to pick out Buckmaster in his chalk-white hat, and
little more to find them both accompanied by a representative cashiered general from the Custom House. As Oates
entered the area with his party, two people said to be the
Parrys came to halt on the other flank. Bowen at once per-
ceived that Shenkin's Law applied to them in the utmost
intensity of its rigour. He wondered if you could have so
much the air of going round looking for something to put a
stop to unless you were really going round doing that.
Waiters arrived with more chairs. The circle expanded to
thirteen persons. Mrs Parry stared round it as though it was
composed of card-sharping perverts. Mr Parry sat rock-like
amid the storm of introductions. Bowen tried to buy some
drinks, conscious of having been fed and made drunk for
free.

'Half a l-l-l-l-l, half a league, half a l-l-l-league,
    Half a ghleague onw-w-w-w-w-w-ward,
All in the v-v-v-v-v-v-valley of mpwdeath
    Rode the s-s-s-s-s-s-s-s-s-s-s ...'

'This chap's marvellous,' Oates said. Rosie had her demure
smile. Bachixa, at Bannion's side, was looking up at him
urgently, perhaps getting ready to break in and ask him to
come and see his motor-bike. De Sousa was falling about in
continuous laughter and darting his big convex eyes from
face to face. He was also nudging his neighbours every
few seconds: they happened to be Isabella Bannion and the
tennis coach. Marchant was staring balefully at de Sousa,

Rosie curiously at Mrs Parry. The latter case gave no real difficulty, for Mrs Parry's nostrils were shaped like tiny mudguards and gave a far more intimate view of the inside of her nose than is at all common. But what was eating Marchant?

As Bowen leant over to ask, Marchant leant over towards him. 'I say, what's that little monkey-faced sod think he's laughing at?'

'At Harry, I imagine,' Bowen said. 'What's wrong with that?'

'I don't like the way he's doing it. And who is he, anyway? I've never seen him before in my life.'

'He's all right, honestly. He doesn't mean anything by it. He always laughs like that, it's a sign of amiability.'

'Maybe, but I don't like the way he's doing it. And who is he, anyway?'

'Half a, half a, er – wait a minute, half a league,
    Half a, what? Oh, half a mile, er, further on,
  All into the, er-um, the – where's my notes?'

'One hundred twenty *escudos*, if you please, sir.'

'Here, you can't pay all that, Garnet, let me split it with you. Oh, all right, them. Noble of you. But listen: you see that little monkey-faced sod over there?'

'*Obrigado* ... What about him?'

'Well, who is he? And what's he think he's laughing at?'

Bannion now sat down to a rattle of applause and much laughing congratulation. Mrs Parry clapped with her hands parallel, like ever such a sweet little girl, and called out: 'Oh Mr Bannion, that was just simply smashing.' De Sousa was almost off his chair, his eyes showing their whites. Bachixa showed his appreciation deliberately, critically, as one who has heard a complicated modern score performed with workmanlike solidity rather than with brilliance. Mr

Parry merely filled his pipe. He had a wooden look on his wooden face.

'Oh by the way,' Oates murmured, 'I don't know whether this is quite the ideal time, but there's something I've been meaning to tell you, if you don't mind.'

'Go ahead, Charlie.' Bowen showed no outward emotion at the suppositions, from an upgrading of board-and-lodging payments to an avowal of love, which came unbidden to his mind.

'I may not see you in the morning and I'm going off to-morrow evening. It's my mother-in-law, you see. You remember I told you she was looking after our baby, little Rosie? Well, she's bringing her back in a few days and she's going to stay on a week or two.'

'I see.' Bowen told himself that if this was leading up to a bed for him in the garage or the hen-run, then Oates, Rosie, little Rosie and mother-in-law, plus any other stray kin of anyone concerned, were going to have had their bloody chips. He would whip up a squad of awful people and pay them to dismember that shagging ginger-coloured German motor-bike. Or he might even bring himself to have the 'serious talk' with Oates that Barbara hourly urged.

'What I want to warn you about is that she's not in very good health. She's liable to have attacks and then who-ever's there has just got to rush out and get a doctor. It might well be you.'

'That's true.' What was truer was that in cases like that it always *was* him; no might about it. And, Christ, wasn't one mother-in-law enough for one man to cope with? Could this fresh one be as bad as his regular one back home? Well, she could and she couldn't.

'That's not all, unfortunately,' Oates was going on.

'Oh?'

'She's basically a nice woman, but she acts rather peculiarly at times. If she takes to you she'll do anything for you, but if not there isn't much you can do to get on the right side of her.'

'Sort of strong likes and dislikes?'

'Well, that kind of thing. And sometimes she flies into terrible rages with people she doesn't like. Of course it doesn't really mean anything, it's just a thing about her. But I thought I'd better warn you; you know, just in case.'

'Thanks, Charlie.' In Bowen's mental projection-theatre an exophthalmic hag with a knife of traditional Portuguese pattern was chasing him round and round Oates's 'garden', for some reason at Chaplin-revival speed and with corresponding intensity of gesture.

'But how would you feel if some brute murdered ... let's say your mother?' Bowen suddenly heard Mr Parry ask Alec Marchant. 'Or ... well, your sister.' Parts of his face, for instance the mouth and eyelids, had come to life while the rest remained log-like. He resembled a Societ chess master, from somewhere like the Uzbek Autonomous Socialist Republic rather than the Russian S.F.S.R., arrived at the bottom board of a multiple game.

'My mother's dead and I haven't got a sister.'

Mr Parry nodded slowly. His mind seemed to be groping back to a parallel manoeuvre at the Tchigorin Memorial Tourney of 1950. This was to be no *blitzkrieg*, after all. 'No,' he pronounced eventually. 'All right. Take your wife, then. How would you feel if some brute murdered your wife?'

'It's very hard to say. Stunned, I should say.'

'Stunned, did you say?'

'Yes. Stunned.'

'You mean ... sort of ... with grief? Stunned with grief?'

'Roughly.'

'Of course you would be,' Mr Parry said, tapping himself here and there in search of his pouch. 'Of course you would be. But when that feeling of being stunned wore off, as it'd be bound to do in time, wouldn't it? I mean ... I don't want you to go and misunderstand me ...'

'No, I won't do that.'

'All right. But ... when it wore off, that feeling of being ... stunned ...'

A kind of cross-facing process brought Harry Bannion in over the top of this. He was saying emphatically: '... So there he's lying now, the poor wee man, with his life fast ebbing away from him, and he carls for his best orange sash, do you know, and the fine flag his younger brother's been carrying on the Twelfth these fifty years and more, with good old King Billy on it crossing of the Boyne and the three drops of water dripping from his horse's hoof ... Do you know?'

Oates, Rosie, de Sousa (laughing noiselessly so as not to miss anything), Bachixa and the tennis coach all did know. At any rate, while remaining expectant, they all five nodded their heads in a satisfied way.

'And then he carls out, "Bring me me drum," and they brings it to him, and then with his last breath he commends his soul to his Maker, for he raises himself up' – with this Bannion got to his feet – 'and he murmurs "TO HELL WITH THE POPE!"' This was yelled at full blast and stopped all conversation in the café. 'And with a wee brave dint on his drum he falls bark, straight into the arms of Jesus.' Bannion also fell back, but into his chair, and added in a normal voice: 'Get away now, you boys round the door.'

There was more uproar, of course, and the tennis coach was for some time most prominent in it. Isabella Bannion smiled another affectionate rebuke at her husband. Bowen admired him very much for telling that story. It had contained a quite legitimately censored version of his own view of His Holiness, and was in all ways what its audience deserved. Though clearly not meant as an anti-papal demonstration, it was far more admirable as such than any of Bowen's own routines, from the study-group earnestness of 'Wouldn't you perhaps agree that politically the Church has often been unfortunate in its choice of allies?' to the beery Fabian don's 'Come on, now, you're not really going to sit there and tell me you take all that stuff seriously, are you?'

Through the ebbing tumult Bowen heard Mr Parry once more raising his voice. He hoped hard that the fellow was a Catholic. He was saying to Marchant: 'Well, there you are, then.' The offended look he was sending towards Bannion and his group mingled with triumph as from having countered his opponent's dangerous-looking (14) o-o ch by (15) Q × R!! The two expressions struggled laboriously for mastery on his totemic face.

'I'm sorry,' Marchant said, 'I must have missed some stage in the argument. Forgive me for being so stupid.'

'All right ... I've at last got you to admit that when this ... stunned feeling wore off, you'd probably want to kill the brute who'd murdered your wife.'

'But I admitted that straight away. And what about it?'

'It's what you anti-hanging blokes won't face up to. All very fine and large to kick up a fuss when they're going to hang some brute who's murdered some poor woman at the other end of England, but it's a different tale to tell when it's your own wife. If that happened you'd be all for hanging the brute.'

A look of incredulous horror came over Alec Marchant's face. He said haltingly: 'But the bloody laws *exist* to *stop* people from *killing* each other *whenever they happen to feel like it.* Don't they?'

Mr Parry smoked his pipe for a time. Bowen was almost sure by now that the fellow must be Cardiff, if not Newport. 'Ah, but that's only your opinion,' Mr Parry said at length.

Marchant got up and began repeating 'Christ Almighty' somewhere in the counter-tenor range. Everybody else immediately got up too and prepared to leave. He tried to stop them, talking about and then vainly trying to order more coffee, a final drink. Meanwhile Bowen found himself face to face with Mr Parry.

'You're from Swansea, aren't you?'

'Llansamlet.' Bowen tried to sound like a Texan asked if he was from Monterrey.

Mr Parry did not say where he was from. He and Bowen had already completed what was to be their only sublunary conversation. Mr Parry turned aside and gave Marchant, now advancing upon him, a kind of diagonal farewell nod, as if to say that the two of them had had a first-class friendly wrangle with, when you came to weigh it up, much good sense talked on both sides. Then he withdrew, wife and all.

Bowen let Marchant express something of what he felt about Mr Parry. The man was a J.P., he said several times. Not long afterwards Bowen found himself standing in the roadway with Bachixa talking to him. Bachixa said: 'Come. I will drive you to the house.'

'Oh, no thank you. My wife . . .'

'We will make the journey very quickly, sir.'

'I'm afraid it's quite out of the question.'

A minute later they were moving on to the main road, heeling over to do so at an angle where Bowen could have touched the ground if he had extended his arm, which he did not. Before they had come upright a gust of wind – a frequent phenomenon, Bowen had noted, in that part of Portugal – caught them and sent them staggering towards a large brightly-lit bus. Bowen had time to see a little bald man (not unlike a Portuguese Mr Parry, only nicer) laughing in it. Then they were past and accelerating freely down a meagre, fluctuating corridor between the two lines of traffic. Bachixa looked over his shoulder to shout: 'Do you like Portuguese coffee or is it for you too strong?'

Bowen pretended to have missed this until he saw that the other's ear was still turned towards him to catch his reply. 'Yes,' he said. 'No. I like it very much.'

Estoril lay behind them, Bowen ruminated, remote, mysterious and immobile, as they said in the books. Words they did not say in all that many books formed at the threshold of his consciousness. He spoke some, employing a quiet, reasonable tone, into the magic of the Lusitanian night. If he lived he would ever afterward work harder, write more of his own stuff, do more with the kids, live in the United Kingdom. In his belly there was a plucking, a knocking, a shifting like the tide coming stealthily in among rock and weed. First adding 'eat and drink less' to his ever-afterward list, he reflected that abroad was held to deepen your knowledge of your compatriots as well as all the other things it was held to do, and felt there might be something in this. In addition, abroad reputedly gave you fresh insight into – wait for it – yourself. So, for that matter, would a sharp go of locomotor ataxia or a visit from the dough-faced Christian physicist who had lived above him in Swansea. And anyway, he already had as much insight into himself as he cared to have.

With a toot and a continuous snuffling rattle, de Sousa drew level with them. He and Bachixa shouted gaily at each other. In the momentary beam of a headlight Bowen saw de Sousa's big bright eye flashing away at him. It was as if de Sousa knew exactly how Bowen felt and was reacting to the knowledge in exactly the right way. Yes, speaking the old lingo was important all right. At that moment Bowen would have given much to be able to shout, across the variegated gulfs between them, some small message of solidarity or vituperation.

12

'These are some ships of the sardine fleet,' Afilhado said, 'restoring their nets after their voyage. Many sardines are eaten by the people here. In the north and central districts, it is cod; here in the south, it is sardines.' His kindly serious face looked rather anxiously round the harbour, weighing up, it seemed, whether to risk overwhelming Bowen with information or to court the danger of leaving him in perplexity on some point. Then he smiled. 'Here is something interesting. These fishermen are singing a sea-shanty as they lay out this large net and then place it in folds. By singing in this way they are able to regulate their movements. I think this must be rare now in England, Mr Bowen.'

Sitting in the little sailing-boat between his sons, Bowen felt impressed and found no reason for not being. The notion that this sort of thing could take place without an invisible accompanying orchestra, without Spencer Tracy and Henry Fonda hanging about or joining in, was a pleasant one, even though very little could be done with that notion once it had presented itself. And if the same thing applied to the authentic toothless boatman who saw to the technicalities of their craft, the Moorish-looking fort that commanded the entrance to the harbour, the undeniably colourful fish-market at the landward end, then it was still worth coming some distance to find that these things were so and not otherwise. Although the scene on view was no more beautiful or significant than, say, a Pimlico bus-garage, yet no conceivable writer or painter (especially painter) could have been trusted to render it honestly: the whole shooting-match would have sunk without trace under the assaults of their 'personal vision', their 'comment', their 'subordination of inessentials'. What gave them the idea that they knew what they meant by an inessential, much less could pick one out? Fair enough; but was it worth coming *something over a thousand miles* to look at this harbour and think these thoughts? Ah, well, now, that was all according, wasn't it?

Afilhado was conferring with the boatman about something. Bowen could not help calling him Afilhado, even though he had worked out that this was not the chap's name, but merely the perfect participle passive of the Portuguese verb cognate with 'affiliate', and could thus only be used with propriety by the Bannions, who had adopted him. They had more or less adopted the five Bowens too, come to that, having extricated them from Oates's establishment and installed them rent-free in a chalet they owned in the mountains that overlooked the coastal plain. Today Harry Bannion had summoned them for lunch, preceding this by the boating party for the male Bowens and a shopping expedition for Barbara under Isabella's guidance. Sandra Bowen was being stuffed and cosseted by the Bannions' maids. Some drinks had already been had that morning; more were promised before the meal and more still would beyond question be had during and after it. It was going to be a nice full day. One of the main snags about abroad was that there was normally nothing to do there, unless indeed you turned your back on reason and went on route-marches round foreign Towers of London and Hampton Courts. As soon as you crossed the sea you stopped having any motive beyond the merest whim for being where you were rather than anywhere else. How different when you were taken abroad by the Army, which imposed on you a purpose outside yourself and provided you with a job, a circle of friends, recognized modes of leisure and a coherent attitude to your surroundings – the very things a civilian traveller had to manage without. Well, for the next few hours at any rate these deprivations were going to lose their bite.

'You notice this ship here, Mr Bowen,' Afilhado's mild voice was saying. 'You notice perhaps it is built in a different fashion from the others. It is higher above the water.'

'Oh, that blue one? Yes, it is different, isn't it?'

'You notice that it has "*Suomi*" painted on its side.'

'So it has.'

' "*Suomi*" means "Finland".'

'Oh yes?'

'It is "Finland" in the Finnish language.'

'That's interesting.'

'It is curious how that ship comes to be here.'

'Yes.' Bowen made a great business of taking out his packet of 20-20-20 miniature cigars: nearly as nice as his Dutch favourites and 8d. for twenty. Afilhado waited politely until he had lit one, then continued:

'Since a year the crew of this ship murdered their captain. The ship was sailing from a port in Morocco. The crew joined together in a conspiracy and carried out this murder. Then they sailed the ship here and surrendered themselves to the authorities, confessing what they had done. They were taken from here to Lisbon so that it was decided what must become of them. The ship remained here and they were taken back to Finland by land. There they experienced a trial for the murder. I cannot say what happened to them.'

'Were they hung?' David and Mark seemed to ask at once.

'I cannot say. I suppose they were imprisoned. But, as you see, Mr Bowen, the ship remains here even now. The captain's father received the ship by the will of the captain. He made the journey here from Finland, because he wished to sell the ship and here there was nobody who might sell the ship for him. In Finland, you know, the ship would be worth much money. But here it is of no use. It is of the wrong shape for the fishing of sardines and so the captain's father cannot sell it. He did not know of this when he came. And he has no money with which to pay the men who should sail it back to Finland for him, and he has no money with which to make his own journey back to Finland. So he remains here, and he has made of the ship his home. He does this for almost a year.'

Bowen said: 'Why did the crew murder the captain?'

'I cannot say. But it seems that he was a very bad captain. Look, Mr Bowen. You can see the captain's father now.'

A fat pig-faced man with thin white hair was walking along the deck of *Suomi*, which they were now passing at a distance of a few yards. He wore a white singlet and shapeless blue trousers, but he reminded Bowen of Mr Binns, the prosperous grocer he saw in the pub at home. The captain's father began gathering over his arm some underclothes which had been hung over a stay to dry. Then the sail of their own boat hid him from view.

'What does he do for a living?' Bowen asked.

'At first he was employed on one of the sardine ships. But he could not learn how to perform that job. And so he is now employed in the fish-market.'

A powerful, useless thrill ran through Bowen. Here was a marvellous story for someone, but not, unfortunately, for him. Only a rather worse or much older writer than himself could tackle it satisfactorily. W. Somerset Maugham (on grounds of age, not lack of merit) was the kind of chap. 'I have a notion that men are seldom what they seem.' Or 'Lars Ericssen' – something like that, anyway – 'was the skipper of a small Finnish cargo vessel. He was a big bronzed man who never looked you directly in the eye. One hot summer off Tangier ...' Mm. A rather worse or much older writer. Well, just say a writer, instead of a man who was supposed to be a writer. That would get it.

They landed soon after that and Bowen stopped half-way up the beach to get the sand off his feet and put on his socks and shoes. Afilhado stepped without fuss into a pair of wet plimsolls – they somehow yielded a plausible harmony with his military-style jacket and clerical collar – and told Bowen a story to tide him over this otherwise rather unrewarding interval.

'So the Father says to his servant, "José, because you are my old trusty servant I will tell you how I can disappear from the street. In that street lives my little lady-friend, but I am the Father and so I cannot knock at her front door. So when I visit her I make like a dog 'owr, owr-owr' and she throws from her window a rope which I climb. Now, José, you understand." Then the next evening the Father goes to the street and he makes 'owr, owr-owr' as he always does. But when he expects the rope to come from the window he hears instead of this someone who makes 'rrrrrrUH, rrrrrrUH.' So the poor Father calls out, "José, you ungrateful man. Only yesterday I am teaching you how to bark, and now you wish to bite me."'

Bowen laughed a great deal. He watched while Afilhado, who felt perhaps that the grown-ups had had things their own way for too long, cracked a successful joke with the boys, using that special sedate affectionateness that priests and nuns always seemed to go in for. It was a pity that the depth and duration of his acquaintance with Afilhado were necessarily so limited. He had felt rather the same way about de Sousa and Bachixa, now evermore sundered from him, and even – a far more arresting achievement – about Carlos Joaquim Cordeiro Oates. Things had had to pile up a good deal to bring Bowen to the point of announcing to that man that their association must terminate: a forty-eight-hour boycott by Barbara, a further slackening of domestic routine, an intimation from Marchant that Oates was charging half as much again as the Pensão Internacional, a qualitative change for the worse in the Oates lavatory, the Bannions' offer of their chalet. Even these might not have sufficed without the sight of Oates riding in after work with a brand-new windshield fixed to his ginger-coloured motor-bike. Filling in time by working out how many bottles of disinfectant that windshield was worth, Bowen had waited for Oates to change his suit jacket for his pyjama jacket – a habit of his on hot evenings – because he could hate him more thus attired. Then he had given notice. After a lot of blinking and creaking and file-consulting and references to the by now legendary Seixas Peres (Olivia's in-laws' Lisbon pal), Oates had said he would need to be paid for two weeks instead of one if his accounts were to balance. Bowen had seen no reason why they should do that at his expense – but still, it had been worth it to say good-bye to that bleeding insect-vivarium Oates called a house. And so off they had gone, the senior Bowens again on speaking terms, the boys asking for a translation of the Lone Ranger in Portuguese, Sandra clutching the dolls which, in a rather pathetic pretence that cordiality was unimpaired, had been pressed upon her by

Rosie and mother-in-law – no swooner or psychotic she, it had transpired, but the sturdiest and most amenable member of the household. It had all been a noteworthy foray into the horrendo-comic, but then, as before, you could probably run into something just as noteworthy, and just as remote from your ordinary life, at five minutes' march from Bowen's parents' house in Llansamlet, nr. Swansea, Glam. It would be harder to write about, that was all.

Resigning himself, perforce, to never knowing what made Oates tick or how he got his shaving-water from the geyser to the wash-basin, Bowen mounted the little hill at Afilhado's side. He admitted to himself now that he had felt rather uneasy in the sailing-boat. Suppose he had been and gone and fallen into the water all of a sudden? A fine thing that would have been. He had thought in the past that a binary system of laziness and conceit accounted fully for all the motions of his life, but of late its orbit had shown perturbations from a third component. This additional body seemed to be fear, and abroad, of course, was what took him to perihelion. It had done it before, in 1944–5, without having to put him in a moment's real danger. He hoped hard that nothing nasty was going to happen on this trip. Well, the recession of the Buckmaster *imbroglio* – they had come south without the chance of seeing him again – was some sort of reassurance there. Good stuff.

'I suppose you have learnt some words of the language since you are in Portugal, Mr Bowen?'

'Oh yes. Not enough to hold a conversation, of course, but I can order drinks and things.'

Afilhado laughed. 'That is important.' He looked like the nice boy who explains things to you at a new school. 'Portuguese is a most interesting language. It is a very pure language. It is derived, you know, from Latin.'

'Like Spanish and French and so on.'

'Yes. But Portuguese is more pure than they are. It is very close to Latin.'

'Closer than Spanish, for instance?'

'Oh, assuredly, much closer.'

'In what way?'

'It is more pure, purer. Altogether a purer language.'

'I see.'

'I give you an example. Portuguese and Spanish are quite different, but they are closely related. It should be possible for a Portuguese person to understand a Spanish person when he speaks. But this is not possible because all Spaniards speak with a very very bad accent. It is altogether impossible to understand them. Now, on the contrary, it is completely possible for the Spaniards to understand the Portuguese, because their accent is very good and because their language is so much purer.'

'Yes, well that does show the difference, I agree.'

'But now I tell you something very stupid, Mr Bowen. All the Spaniards pretend that it is impossible for them to understand the Portuguese. They say, "Ah no no no, we cannot understand you." But this is what they pretend. They say it is altogether impossible for them to understand the Portuguese because they do not wish to understand. In the reality they understand quite well.'

'How absurd of them.'

'Is it not absurd? But then I am afraid this is typical of the Spaniards. Of course, I have many good Spanish friends, you know. But on these questions they are sometimes very absurd. I think it is impossible for them to forget some events of history. On the last occasion when a battle was carried on between the two nations, the Portuguese were very greatly victorious, although their army was altogether smaller. This is since several centuries, but it is

·impossible for the Spaniards to forget it. But on the contrary, this is not a serious matter. At present I think the Spaniards and the Portuguese understand each other very well. This is a service of our Dr Salazar. He has performed much work to assist the two nations to understand each other.'

They reached the terrace of the Bannions' house, which overlooked the harbour. Here, under a capacious umbrella, drinks were drunk and olives stuffed with anchovies eaten. Lunch was all Bowen had foreseen, and more. There was soup, shellfish stew, roast pork, chicken, plum pudding, fruit, cheese, cakes, sweets, chocolates, coffee, red wine, white wine, port, brandy, madeira, cigars. About four o'clock Bowen, breathing shallowly, got himself into the Morris. He thanked everybody a lot and would have liked to go on doing so for much longer. This kind of thing, at any rate, was nowhere to be found in Llansamlet, nr. Swansea, Glam.

Barbara's shopping trip had been a success. She had bought food for the family as a whole, clothing and footwear for herself and the children, drink (including Lisbon gin at 11s. the large bottle) for her husband. There was change from the money she had been given, too: not much, but some. Isabella Bannion had contrived to slip in presents for each of the five. On the drive back to the mountains Bowen relapsed into a torpor. It was some protection against noticing too continuously how the day's satisfactions had imparted vivacity and fire to Barbara's driving, against picturing too distinctly how they would look with the bonnet in accordion-pleats, being towed God knew where by one of the local bullock-carts. He had familiarized himself with the bullock-cart image during the southern part of their long drive down from Lisbon the previous week; during the northern part it had necessarily been a mule-cart image. The general idea, however, was the same.

Arriving at the chalet without mishap, Barbara dropped Bowen there while she went on into the village to pick up the mail. It was now his task to pump up water from the well into the tank to provide for the making of tea, the preparation of baths, etc. He liked this job: it made him feel all son-of-the-soil without much exertion. During it he talked cheerfully to the hobbled piglet the Bannions had given them, trying to forget that it was destined to become roast pork in a few weeks. Afterwards he greeted the mangy stray cat and emaciated stray dog adopted by Barbara on her arrival, then went to see if the toad was still in his crevice under the garden wall. He was, looking in excellent trim, but as usual trying to pretend he wasn't there. Bowen went into the house, where others of God's creatures were buzzing phrenetically about. He got going with the fly-squirter; it was wonderful having one of his own after the meagre goes with Oates's instrument he had been allowed. He gave his and Barbara's bedroom special attention. Last night he had sat up in bed reading Elizabeth Taylor and squirting the enemy by turns, thinking this a happy combination of pastimes, but Barbara had objected to the way dying insects kept falling into her hair and on to her face and bare shoulders, so he had had to stop. There was always some snag about out-of-the-way pleasures.

He went into the sitting-room, where his work-table was. Here were grounds, he thought, for some complacency and self-congratulation. The article for *See* magazine and two others lay there in draft- or substantial note-form; a 1200-word review of a work on the Bloomsbury group, sent to him at Oates's, awaited only its covering letter; *Teach Him a Lesson* had got on to page 35; a couple of sheets of jottings about Buckmaster/Strether were ready in case. Oh, not bad at all. And beyond the typewriter stood a more reliable aid to well-being: a full bottle of *medronha* with a kind of tree inside it. A local liqueur resembling *calvados*, but made from an arboreal strawberry-like fruit, it was an excellent nightcap, especially after a few glasses of *vinho tinto* and a port or two and a brandy or two. But the sight of it at this moment must have had some triggering effect on Bowen's alimentary canal. From inside him came a sound like that of distant but approaching horsemen. He ran into the lavatory.

When he came out he found Barbara just arriving with the post. She said: 'Nothing from Mummy. I hope she's all right.'

'Of course she is. You'll hear tomorrow. She'll only just have got your letter telling her the new address.'

'I wish I'd sent it to her sooner.'

'You couldn't have done. You wrote the moment you knew.'

'Perhaps she's sent one to Oates's place.'

'Well, if she has he'll forward it.'

She did her vigorous head-shake, inhaling and shutting her eyes. 'I wouldn't be too sure of that.'

'Oh, nonsense, he wouldn't do anything he thought was nasty.'

'What about that extra cash he took off us?'

'He didn't think that was nasty. He thought he was entitled to that.'

'But it was nasty, whatever he thought about it.'

'That doesn't make any difference; he didn't think it was nasty.'

'I think it makes all the difference,' she said stoutly.

'Well yes, in general it does, but we're talking about Oates doing or not doing things he thinks are nasty.'

'I can't see why that should be special.'

'It isn't special, dear. All I'm saying is that if he thinks a thing's nasty he doesn't do it, probably.'

'But surely the important thing is that he does do nasty things when he doesn't think they're nasty.'

'I was only trying to establish . . .'

'Sandra, leave those things alone in there.' She sped out of the room.

Bowen sighed, then grinned, then stopped grinning. Here was a letter addressed in Oates's neat writing. A demand for more money? Ha ha. Ha ha. Ha ha ha ha ha ha ha ha ha ha.

He ripped it open to find what must be a cable inside. Oates had written on it in pencil: *Sorry this is delayed but I was away shooting at the week-end and Rosie didn't know your address. Do hope everything turns out alright. Kindest regards – C.J.C.O.* The sender of the cable was Mrs Knowles's next-door neighbour and the text ran: PLEASE RETURN IMMEDIATELY MOTHER VERY ILL.

13

Bowen sat on the veranda of Buckmaster's house, a glass of madeira before him. He was thinking about Barbara, whom he had seen off on the plane for London, together with the kids, ten days earlier. Arranging their air passages, plus fixing up to get the car taken back on its own by sea, plus cancelling four steamer tickets and changing to a single berth for his own return trip, had given firm promise of coalescing into the most mountainous bum that had ever confronted him, but just in time he had remembered Bennie Hyman's agent in Lisbon. The agent, on whom somebody had done a splendid job of combining de Sousa and Bachixa, had smiled and made three phone calls. The tone of the first one had been of a cringing self-abasement, of the second a bawling maniacal fury, of the third an insultingly cynical detachment. He had used his face and whole body and all four limbs as well as just his voice, reducing the Bowen children to an immobile silence they had not shown since leaving their television set. After the performance the agent, once more de Sousa-Bachixa, had smiled a second time and asked if the lady could wait until tomorrow morning. The matters of the car and the passenger berths he would, if permission were given, order his secretary to deal with the next day.

After the airlift Bowen had got on a train and gone back down south, where the Bannions had pleaded to be allowed to put him up for a week. It had been a period of wonderful stability, free from the slightest threat of encounters with the unmanageable, full of food and drink and even work. At the end of it the Bannions, with profuse apologies for not being able to go on supporting him indefinitely, were to depart for a month's stay in Northern Ireland. Room had however been found for him, should he want it, at what Harry Bannion described as 'Afilhado's priests' place' along at Faro. Details of this place proved hard to extract. Bowen's imagination flickered between a four-star monastery with chanting and flagellation, where he might have to sleep in a cell or something, and a sort of hieratic training unit in Nissen huts, where he might have to do fatigues or something. Alternatively there was the Pensão Familial down the road, but this would cost money. Money was something Bowen currently lacked. His purse already thinned by Oates's depredations, he had had to lay out all he had on the airline tickets and borrow from Harry Bannion as well. The shipping company's refund had covered the loan and put him some distance into the black, but not comfortably far, especially since he had decided to make a shot at repaying the Bannions' kindness by giving Afilhado a donation for his priests' place, where no doubt an extra censer-chain or bayonet-sack was always acceptable. In the circumstances he could hardly borrow any more. Why hadn't he gone back with Barbara? Everywhere he turned there was a reason for asking that. He was in the middle of asking it when the phone rang one night and Buckmaster came through on the line.

Yes, on his return from Coimbra he had had Bowen's kind letter explaining about their move. Yes, wanting very much to see them again he had rung up the mountain post office and local knowledge of the Bannions had done the rest. What, Bowen's family had had to return to England? What damnably hard luck. The news of the sick lady was reassuring? Excellent. And what were Bowen's plans now? Leaving there at the end of the week? Going where? But goodness gracious there could be no possible question but that Bowen should come and spend the rest of the time with him. No, he was sorry but he simply was physically unable to contemplate taking no for an answer. His car would meet the train in Lisbon.

And so Bowen had come to be where he was now, uneasy but in quite tolerable shape on the whole, sitting on Buckmaster's veranda with a glass of madeira before him and thinking about Barbara. At least officially he was thinking about Barbara, but thoughts of Buckmaster had a way of keeping on breaking in. The line of least resistance, backed up by cloudy visions of gain, had brought him here, rather against both his better judgement and his conscience. His better judgement had ceased to offer effective opposition when it became clear that Buckmaster was after all a tolerable companion: his grandiosity was balanced by his eagerness to please, his gratitude for any interest shown

141

in him, and his insufficiently keen but still impressive anxiety not to be boring. These last qualities had had the effect of bringing up the noise-level of conscience a bit, but Bowen had given that the kick in the teeth by promising himself (i) never to reveal anything that might damage Buckmaster's claim to be Strether; (ii) if that claim was finally upheld, never to publish a word of his now-voluminous notes on the old boy without his consent. That looked like that, but it wasn't quite, because it really would be very interesting to know if Buckmaster actually was Strether. And on that one he had no more evidence than when he got out of the Morris on his first visit.

Before Bowen could finally switch his brain on to Barbara, Buckmaster came apologetically on to the veranda. He put the bottle of madeira and a glass on the little table, then sat down opposite Bowen and poured himself a drink. He was sound on the drink question. Smiling affably, he cleared his throat. 'The . . . the calling of the literary critic or reviewer,' he said. 'Would you rate it highly, my friend?'

His habit of calling Bowen his friend like this really was rather terrible, but hard to block. Bowen drank some of his own madeira as a means of keeping things at arm's length. 'No, I don't think so,' he said. 'Why?' He wondered what he was in for this time. Buckmaster couldn't, or perhaps wouldn't, converse; he held forth instead in a series of essays. They had had reflections of an expatriate, the gastronome in Iberia, the economic consequences of the peace, Jane Austen: the first Victorian?, love and marriage (a shortish one, that), Portugal – i: the country, Portugal – ii: the people, *Far From the Madding Crowd* revalued and, this very lunch-time, the nature and significance of literary creation. Almost throughout that one, and for long stretches of the Austen and Hardy pieces, Bowen had been expecting Buckmaster to make a noise like an asterisk and direct him to the foot of an aural column where there would be details of title, author, publisher and net price. The *Sunday Times* would absolutely eat this chap.

'Criticism' – the lecturette was well into its stride now – 'is doubtless a perfectly valid manifestation of the sensibility and the understanding, as the author of *The Spirit of the Age*, along with Elia in his less introspective moments, have testified in such happy abundance. Their work was creative, in spite of the fact – perhaps, indeed, because of it – that it seldom bore much relation to the avowed objects of their inquiry. These, however, were mostly dead and buried: a vitally important point. All criticism, in my view, even that which we call creative, is an activity of a lower order than creative work in the more usual sense, and we see the relevance of that view when we apply it to criticism of the living. I may have mentioned that I instructed my publisher to send me no reviews of my work as it appeared. My reason was that I needed no false praise which might mislead me with regard to my merits, and – more particularly – no abuse which might discourage me. You will remember that Gabriel Rossetti, whom my father had several times the privilege of meeting in the great man's last years, was reduced to poetic silence for half a decade as a direct result of ill-natured attacks in the public print. These journalistic outpourings are now deservedly forgotten, and their only effect upon posterity has been to deprive it of a number of poems we should not have chosen to be without, to put it no higher.'

'Very much the same sort of thing happened in Elgar's career,' Bowen blurted out before he could stop himself. He tried to cheapen it with 'So a fellow was telling me, anyway,' but only succeeded in making himself sound modest. A moral failure on this scale came about through attending too closely to what people were saying. Those perishing

143

vodka martinis at the International Musicians' Club that time must have weakened his protective shell without him noticing. He had thought that the film-composer chap who was buying them all had merely been boring him. And now here was this gross betrayal into non-ironical cultural discussion. When he got home he would wait for Barbara to bring up the topic of integrity and then announce that he was going to cancel the *New Statesman*.

'Madeira is not perhaps the ideal liquor on a hot afternoon like this,' Buckmaster said.

'A bit heavy, you think?'

'Between meals, yes, I do. I recommend a bottle of cold beer.'

'That sounds an excellent suggestion.'

'Two *cerjevas*, then. Excuse me a moment.'

When Buckmaster had gone, Bowen sat up very straight, his heart beating. There had been something striking about that oration on criticism. It was not just that he had been a trifle unfair to the *Sunday Times*, that the proper people to eat Buckmaster were the powers at our older universities, where he would be a valuable counterblast to clever young men like F. R. Leavis. More than that. Could a man who had really written all those novels really be bounded by James and Conrad and Edith Wharton and Meredith, could he really not have noticed anything that had happened since? And wasn't Buckmaster's whole attitude that of a reader rather than a writer, wasn't his whole *persona* arranged on the lines of what a reader would expect a writer to be like? And, if this was so, wasn't the non-production of any Strether document an incredibly fishy evasion? Why was it that no pal of Buckmaster's had been produced or mentioned as booked to appear, nobody who might give away that he wasn't Strether if he wasn't Strether? Why was it all so *difficult*? A burst of neurotic frustration rocked

Bowen in his seat: it was like putting a new ribbon in his typewriter to the accompaniment of a ringing telephone, a waiting taxi and a full bladder.

Just then a car became audible and soon afterwards rounded the corner of the dusty track that led up to the house. It was a big open car, glittering fiercely in the sun, and it contained a man and a girl. Before it reached the paved yard below him Buckmaster reappeared, carrying two bottles of beer and two glasses on a tray. 'I thought I heard –' he said. His voice broke off instantly and, banging the tray down on the slatted table, he strode to the veranda rail. Bowen saw the man in the car, who was driving it, raise a brown hand in greeting and flash a smile.

Buckmaster's feet moved agitatedly. He looked back and forth between his visitors and Bowen, as if trying to gauge the effect each party might have on the other. His mouth, no longer sensitive, hung down in a slack and rather pitiable way. Bowen stopped himself from asking if he was all right. The slamming of the car doors below made them both jump. Buckmaster looked hard at Bowen for a moment, this time with the unmistakable air of one visualizing another's response to some plan or hint. He said in a precarious undertone: 'This is a man I used to know slightly some time ago. Not, I fear, a very prepossessing character.'

'Oh, pity,' Bowen said as bluffly as he could.

The new arrivals could be heard laughing and chatting gaily to each other as they mounted the wooden stair. Buckmaster hurried forward to meet them, blocking Bowen's view when they reached the veranda. A pang of almost unbearable excitement, as well-defined as a pang of fear, displaced all his uneasiness when he heard the man say in a jovial, lightly-accented voice: 'Why, hallo, John.' My God, the whole thing might be settled one way or the other in the next couple of minutes.

'I hope you don't mind us just to pop in like this,' the man was going on, 'but we were making a visit at Lisbon and thought we'd look you up. You don't know my friend, I think.' Bowen made out the friend's name as Emilia (or Amelia) something, the something containing one specimen each of the *sh* and the *owng* which seemed compulsory in all Portuguese words of more than one syllable. 'And how is your health these days, John old man?'

Still talking, his hand on Buckmaster's shoulder, the man made his way along the veranda. He didn't look in the least unprepossessing, in fact for a man of at least fifty he was remarkably handsome and healthy-looking, so that his lilac-grey suit and thinly-striped white tie seemed further manifestations of well-being. This quality he radiated in full measure, either not noticing or deciding to ignore Buckmaster's nervousness, which hadn't moderated at all. Between them they still blocked Bowen's view of the girl. They put this right when they reached his chair and he got politely to his feet.

When he saw her he had some trouble in choking back the kind of loud bass groan with *tremolo* that his R.A.F. friend (the Cader Idris one) used to utter at the sight of even moderately attractive women. There was nothing moderate about Emilia/Amelia. She was tall and managed to be stately and agile-looking at the same time, just as her unmade-up mouth protruded as well as being slightly thin. Under a crinkly white hat she had the darkest fair hair he had ever seen. Her wide-skirted dress and lace gloves were white too, and might have been taken a moment before out of a plastic wrapper, like the rest of her. That was clever with all this heat and dust. It was hard to imagine her doing a domestic task, unless giving orders to servants counted as that. With all this she had the cheek to look unassuming, cheerful and even friendly. She must have been about twenty but, as the R.A.F. friend would have put it, you could never tell with these foreign bints.

After staring at her for what seemed like a quarter of an hour or so, Bowen allowed himself to be introduced. Poor old Buckmaster's still unabated nervousness prevented Bowen from fully enjoying the girl, which was a pity in a way, but if rightly viewed was also desirable.

'Well now, John, tell us of all you've been doing,' the Portuguese man said jauntily, looking round for chairs.

'Of course. I wonder, however ...'

'Ah, a nice cool beer. Just what I fancy to have.'

'Would you mind very much ...' Buckmaster said to Bowen with evident difficulty. 'I have some urgent business to discuss with Dr Lopes here, which would I fear prove excessively tedious for you young people. Perhaps you, my friend, would like to take the *senhorita* down to the bar at the corner for something refreshing?'

'I'm afraid she doesn't speak a good deal of English,' Lopes said, gazing interestedly at Buckmaster. 'And here on the table this beer ...'

'Nonsense, I'm sure they'll manage to get on perfectly well. Would you be so good, my friend?'

His friend would just have to be so good. 'Of course, I'd be very glad to, if the *senhorita* has no objection.' It must all have come about through drinking that madeira, a nice little wine really, and even, as the previous evening had established, a nice big wine if you drank enough of it, hardly tasting of British sherry at all. Courtly foreign grace was what it gave you.

Meanwhile, Lopes had shrugged his shoulders and was saying a few sentences in Portuguese to the girl, who looked amiably from face to face. The last sentence was delivered in a sharper tone than the others and was followed by a grin directed at Buckmaster. The old boy didn't notice; he could scarcely keep still with impatience. The girl nodded and smiled at Bowen. As they moved away he heard Buckmaster say something loud and expostulatory in Portuguese. It made Lopes, laugh, whatever it was.

In the next few minutes it became apparent that the operating staff at the great telephone exchange – or, more precisely perhaps, the fair-sized provincial switchboard – which was Bowen's brain were a bit under strength that day. At any rate, the circuits had begun to get clogged. Buckmaster could hardly be Strether now, not after hallo John, used to know him slightly plus urgent business, and you young people eff off and no questions welcomed. There was, naturally, a multitude of possible innocent explanations, all equally likely and unlikely, that must be chewed over at leisure, or could be by someone possessed of the requisite chewing-over fitments. That let him out, he felt. And then there was this Emilia girl. So far she had seemed adequately occupied in just striding along buxomly at his side, but it was too much to hope that this would keep her happy indefinitely. The years in London had helped him to evolve a shameful oh-really-how-incredible kind of patter adapted for female secretaries and journalists, for editresses, for real or supposed poetesses and even paintresses. It would be no good on this occasion. What would be? Suddenly he got the brilliant idea of *asking* Emilia if she knew anything *about Buckmaster*. He gave her a smile to assure of his good intentions and, if at all possible, his sanity. Then he said: 'You know Mr Strether well, *senhorita*?'

'*Como?*' she asked. It was a word he had got to know well.

'Senhor S-t-re-ther ... you know him?'

'Oh yes,' she said with radiant blandness, as if he had told her that an island was a piece of land entirely surrounded by water.

'Doctor Lopes ... *vieux amigo de* Senhor S-t-re-ther?'

'Lopes – oh yes.' This time she laughed and looked rallying at him. Perhaps he had somehow impugned the man's virility, or else implied that he judged it to be formidable. Whichever it was, it seemed best to leave off while he was still winning.

They turned into the road and walked along the narrow verge. Near at hand a considerable display of foreign vegetation was going on: a dehydrated affair with horny yellow-and-green leaves arranged like the spokes of a wheel grew plentifully, along with more than one sort of extraterrestrial-looking cactus, and the intervening earth, reddish in colour, was almost covered with a matt-finish creeper which would have seemed more natural creeping up something, instead of just along. Further away there were some pine-trees, if they could be that in these latitudes. Perhaps they could be, for he thought he remembered Buckmaster telling him that the nut-like things they ate instead of crisps with their madeira were really pine-needles of a kind, not nuts. Interesting, that. Well, in a way. He must remember not to mention this custom if ever Portugal, madeira nuts or pine-trees came up in conversation after his return to the U.K.

They rounded a bend and a gang of men working on the road were to be seen, just beyond a triangular metal sign that showed a stylized silhouette of such a man. After a moment the Emilia girl touched Bowen on the arm, smiled, pointed with her neatly-hatted head and more or less drew him away from the road into the vegetation area. The going was not easy and he wondered about her stockings. Still, Christ, a girl like this would have a couple of hundred gross more pairs at home, and probably an emergency pack in the car. The same kind of thing must apply to her dresses. The only problem was why they had left the road. Probably it was the road-workers. After about ten hours in this sun being showered with dust from upper-class cars, they could hardly have been blamed for mocking or abusing an upper-class girl in the company of one who, without being upper-class to any immoderate or reprehensible extent, was an obvious foreign swine.

There was shade under the trees, but more heat rather than less. When the girl showed signs of thinking it time to bend their course back to the road, Bowen moved into the lead and took them deeper into the wood. Why, whatever did he want to go and do a thing like that for? All at once he had been struck by the theory that, since he thought he remembered the road taking a big loop round about here, striking through these woodland glades would actually save them time and trouble. This seemed to him important.

Soon they came upon a small clearing where there was turf as short and close as on an English golf-course. Here Bowen halted. So did Emilia, resting a hand on the branch of a convenient tree in a queenly manner. Then she looked at him with the kind of coldness that made him begin to be afraid she might suddenly start doing a dance for him, singing harshly and unintelligibly and with bags of stamping, hand-clapping and finger-clicking, even with a spot or two of the old *olé*. That was Spanish, he knew, but it might easily prove to be Portuguese as well; you could never be sure. To obviate any of that, he took out his Players (2s. the large packet in Lisbon) and offered them. 'Have a fag, tosh,' he said.

She took one docilely. When she bent to his match he saw that her eyelashes grew thick and parallel all the way along, not in the little criss-crossing groups most girls had, then he glanced away over her shoulder, studying the nearby tree with a botanist's intentness. He really could not have her glancing up at him under those lashes of hers. At the same time he noticed she smelt odd, not with any known female smell nor in the least unpleasantly, but rather as if she had picked up some kitchen ingredient or essence by mistake for the scent-bottle. He had often thought that culinary perfumes – ginger, mango chutney, fried onions – might make a nice change, and this cinnamon or cloves of hers certainly did. It made her no less attractive, anyhow. The same held for the way she put her hand on his while he lit her cigarette.

He lit his own, sat down on the dry grass, blew out a shred of tobacco. He felt, and doubtless looked, like a Bank Holiday tripper in the Forest of Dean. A moment later Emilia helped this on by capping his sniff with a rumbling, snoring one of her own. She too sat down, first carefully examining the ground.

Well chum, Bowen thought, what goes? So far, by an internal holding of telescope to blind eye, he had been keeping off what he was up to. Still keeping off it, what did she think he was up to or ought to be up to? He wished, as often in the past, that he was a really mature man who 'knew' things like that 'by instinct'. He tried to draw a mental picture of someone who looked like Emilia and who 'was just waiting for you to try it on so she could slap your face', and then of someone who looked like Emilia and who 'was bloody sitting up and begging for it'. Both pictures were highly plausible and resembled each other even more closely than they resembled Emilia. Less immediate pictures now presented themselves. One was of Lopes 'taking one look and seeing what had happened' and stabbing him. Another was of some uniformed employee of Dr Salazar blowing his whistle at the pair of them. A third was of a Chilean short-story writer he had met at a party saying:

'In my home town there are just the ones who know they've got it and the ones who don't yet know they've got it.' That was a specially vivid picture, and in some curious way it modified what he was up to. He was doing very nicely, thank you, just puffing his fag and blowing smoke at the various circling insects.

But he could hardly just go on doing that. '*O sol*,' he said to Emilia, pointing up. '*Bom*.'

'*Sim*,' she said, laughing in a very healthy, out-of-doors way. '*Muito bom*.'

'What? Oh yes, that's right. *Muito bom*.'

She went on laughing, then checked herself and said severely: '*Escute*.' She put her forefinger on Bowen's lapel: '*A jaquêta*.'

'What? Oh, I get you. *A jaquêta*.'

She touched his tie: '*A gravata*.'

'*A gravata*.'

'*A camisa*.'

'*A camisa*. Are you sure that's right?' He checked himself at the last possible moment from breaking wind; some part of his mind must have been reasoning that since he would be doing it in English she wouldn't understand. 'Sorry. *As calças*.'

Her laughter, which had already returned, became almost continuous when they got on to her clothes. He wondered if the parts of the body were next. He put his arm (*o brasso?*) round her shoulders (*as epaulas?*) and touched her warm dry brown skin. Soon she was leaning against him and had laid a forearm across his knee. She had also taken off her hat. When she stopped laughing and turned her face towards him, he saw that she had slight hollows under her cheekbones and her tortoiseshell hair had fallen across her brow. These things made her look tender and meek, but not innocent.

He put both arms round her. Lopes, Salazar's henchman, the Chilean *homme de lettres*, were rendered unavailable. He remembered his R.A.F. friend saying of foreign bints not that you could never tell, but that they were bloody all for it. He kissed Emilia. Her lips were firm and straight and her mouth smelt slightly of wine and garlic. He felt he was enough of a citizen of the world now not to mind that.

14

Just as Emilia's shoulders touched the grass Bowen had the feeling that someone had pushed a blunt red-hot needle hard into his flesh between his trouser-cuff and the top of his sock. Bounding up with a yell, he had time to see a thing with stripes like a wasp, only a good bit bigger, buzzing away towards the undergrowth. He got it beautifully with a great swingeing kick before the worst of the pain got him. He stooped down, gasping and wincing. When Emilia burst into an uproar of foreign laughter, he did his best to join in. He was succeeding quite creditably when, a couple of minutes later, they moved off, although his sting was still sodding painful. In that time the contact between them had been limited to her pressing on the affected place a large medallion with an olden-days chap riding a horse on it which she wore round her neck. Even then he hadn't been able to watch her doing it, not having eyes in the back of his head. In a way he felt content: even the most inordinately mature of men would surely find himself physically and morally incapacitated for a time after a sting from a bastard of a hornet. And, since he could now remember that he had a wife, it was an enormous relief not to have done anything much to Emilia. But he had wanted to do a great deal and had been going to. It was sad to no longer have his cake, in a way, and yet not have eaten it. On the other hand, though, Barbara was never going to know anything about this, so there was no need whatever to worry.

He brushed Emilia's dress down for her. He thought it looked clean enough to keep Lopes's knife in his pocket. As he limped off beside her she said surprisingly: 'We drink.'

'Yes, that's what we do.'

Ten minutes later they were sitting outside the café listening to a peasant swearing at his mule. Bowen found it surprisingly easy to gather that that was what the peasant was doing. His tone and gestures helped a lot. Some men inside the café, who were playing billiards on a peculiar pocketless table, looked over at him and laughed. Emilia laughed too, glancing at Bowen without archness. He touched her hand affectionately, thinking what a nice girl she was and how sad it would be when the time came to say good-bye to her. His leg was only itching now, too. When the old woman who threw up the drinks arrived he tried asking for champagne and, after some by-play with shum-pugg-ner, shahm-pahn-yay and so on, got it. It was Portuguese champagne and went down like mother's milk: he bucked up at the thought that here was yet another field in which French claims to supremacy proved to be unfounded. Emilia made many signs of appreciation as she drank, which was impressively thoughtful of her, considering how many hogsheads of the stuff old Lopes and probably several others must have poured down her throat. He wished he were taking her out to dinner that night.

They were just pouring out the last of the bottle when Lopes turned up. 'I see you've been doing yourselves pretty well,' he said boisterously from the driving-seat. 'I do wish I could join you and have a real drink-up together, only that

I've said we shan't be very late home. Thank you for look-ing after Emilia.' He beamed at Bowen – ironically! There was no way of knowing.

Lopes opened the door for Emilia and she got gracefully into the car. Bowen felt the scene impressing itself on its memory; a nice bit of background music, violins and things, was audible from the wireless in the café. It would have been easy to give in to sentimental melancholy, but his leg was stinging again as well as itching. And something was nagging at his mind, something to do with Buckmaster, something that Emilia had said. But what could an amorous language-lesson have to do with the man who either was or was not the one indisputably major talent to have arisen since the death of that crazy Polish scribbling sea-dog? What, indeed?

He shook hands with Lopes. 'Good-bye, Bowen old man. Nice to have met you. All the best.'

He shook hands with Emilia. 'Good-bye,' she said, un-conscious of how nicely she said it. Her thickly-fringed eyes flashed a little signal at Bowen. That was thoughtful of her too.

The car moved off slowly for a few yards, then got going with a monstrous roar. Emilia waved an elegant gloved hand as they rounded the bend. Bowen strolled back to the table and finished up the champagne before starting back to Buckmaster's. He wondered what it was that Lopes had pulled a couple of inches out of his pocket, just far enough to show Emilia, before he accelerated. It had looked like money. But it couldn't have been. And why shouldn't it have been? And so what? He was going to dismiss all that from his mind and think about Barbara.

Why hadn't he gone back with Barbara? This was an-other of the questions he was sure he would never be sure about. There was the fact that she had insisted he stayed on and 'finished his holiday'. There was the fact that, as he felt at the time, he ought to prove to himself that temporary separation from his wife and her support was not immediately fatal to him. There was the fact that being on hand while she nursed her mother was certain to be as profoundly and frenziedly nasty as anything short of armed assault that could happen to him abroad: Barbara's transformation back into Barbara Knowles, instead of being partial as it was on her ordinary contact with her mother, would become complete. He would have to become Mrs Bowen as well as Mr Bowen, at any rate in dealing with the children, and Mr Knowles on top of that, replacing his late father-in-law as a bulwark against the canvassers, the collectors of discarded clothing, the friends with gifts of allotment-grown vegetables or personally-landed fish, the furnishers wanting to measure the three-piece suite for new loose covers, the milkmen and window-cleaners demanding payment, the bell-pushing schoolchildren, all the diverse grades and categories of those who perpetually milled around on that uncanny little porch with the arrow-slits and stained-glass windows. All that and Barbara impersonating her mother thrown in. Christ. At this distance the fact of what it would be like at Mrs Knowles's far outweighed the fact that had seemed so important to him ten days ago, *viz.* that to accompany his family back to England he would have to get into an aeroplane with them, and a foreign aeroplane at that, and without the inducement of that life-contract with the *Times Literary Supplement* either. Mm. Still, all that plane stuff was just a joke really.

Many and good as might be the reasons for not being with Barbara at the moment, he felt lonely without her. He also felt, a rather surprising and discreditable amount of the time, like a sailor about to go on leave, a condition

which the passes with Emilia had sharpened to that of a
sailor just getting really started on his leave. Since his marriage he had never spent more than a few days away from
Barbara. So it was no wonder that he missed her. Perhaps it
had been worth coming abroad to be got into this instruc-
tive situation. But wait a minute, she'd had all three of the
children in hospital, hadn't she? Hadn't he missed her then,
in a way that visiting-hours only made worse? One of the
insidious effects of abroad was to delude you into thinking
that there were some things you had to come abroad in
order to find out. He had squashed that one pretty
effectively, he remembered thinking, a couple of times
already. And yet here it was again. It just showed how careful you had to be.

He hoped that, if he now put to himself the point that
he hated bloody abroad, it would not be taken as implying
any disrespect to the Portuguese. Considering their main-
land domicile they had been very good to him. They had, it
was true, given his large bowel a run for its money and
made with the insects rather a lot, but they had not tried
to knife him or rob him or break his health down at all
permanently. This self-restraint, however, could not alter
the essential abroadness of the place, the things it must
share with millions of square miles between here and Istan-
bul. All that sun, which made you set out to be colourful
and wonderful instead of keeping quiet and getting on with
the job. All that geography and biology, which made you
behave as if you had invented the country instead of just
living in it. All those buildings, either violently architectural
and historical or else token and temporary. All that wasted
space. All that air of maturity, lack of nervousness and
doubt, devotion to serious shouting argument or dedicated
gaiety, naturalness which was always an actor's naturalness. All those revving motor-bikes, all those touts, all that

staring – which in England would be the mindless inquisitiveness of those whose greyly uniform lives were nourished on mere sensation, but in the sunny South was a frank, free, healthy, open, uninhibited curiosity.

Walking along the track towards Buckmaster's, Bowen burst into song (tune: *She Was Poor But She Was Honest*):

'See him gulping *vinho verde*,
  Scoffing filthy goat's-milk cheese,
Puffing fags of scent and mule-shit,
  While he searches for his fleas,
But he tells 'em '*Obrigado*',
  Full of courtly foreign grace,
'Cos he's got his homeward voucher,
  Safely locked up in his case.'

Buckmaster met him on the veranda. 'You delivered the man Lopes's companion to him?'

'Yes, they're away now.'

'I am much relieved. The man affected to believe he had a claim on me and became abusive when I questioned it. There was some protracted unpleasantness. Eventually I was forced to settle with him so as not to be further persecuted. It was in order to spare you enforced participation in such a scene that I asked you to withdraw. I hope I gave no offence by my abruptness.'

'Not in the least, I quite understand. But you should have let me stay and give you a hand with things.'

'Thank you, my friend. I leave you to yourself until dinner-time. Some *mail* awaits you on the table in the passage.'

Bowen fetched it and sat on the veranda to read it. Apart from the stuff that Oates and/or Bannion had redirected, there was a letter from Barbara which had come straight here.

Dearest Garnet,

How are you, bogey? Been thinking of you a lot. Things aren't back to normal here yet but I should be home in time to straighten up before you arrive. Mummy is wonderful after all she's been through and the rest's done her a lot of good but I'm still worried about her eating, she doesn't seem to fancy anything much. The Dr says the nerves of her stomach are overstrained and only complete rest and quiet will do that any good but a week should see it through. I must say she's been absolutely marvellous, it can't be any fun for her being so active normally being on her back all the time but she's been wonderfully cheerful chattering away almost like she always does, interested in everything, you've really got to hand it to her ...

Bowen conducted a brief inner debate on the topic of what he would most like to hand Mrs Knowles, then sank into a reverie about her, both in isolation and as she affected him. No ailment short of tetanus, he could avouch, would keep her mouth shut. It grieved him that Barbara couldn't see this. What also gave him cause to mourn was the way his relations with his mother-in-law were so resolutely taking their prescribed place in the comic-postcard aspect of his life's odyssey. They followed upon, and emphasized the unity of, the lodgings and kippers, the beer-ups, the sex-oriented days on the beach and muffed encounters on sofas that had played so large a part in his bachelorhood. He could just see himself, shrunk to half Barbara's stature, leering horribly at a globular-bottomed girl on a tandem or, red-nosed and with half-unmoored collar, being hit over the head by Barbara with a rolling-pin. And why was there *so much* about his *mother-in-law* in a letter addressed to *him*?

Well, fair play, the old girl had been ill and Barbara was her daughter, you couldn't get away from that. No, especially the second half of it. He wondered how seriously the old girl had been ill. Pretty seriously, to be prepared to break up the holiday of a daughter she undoubtedly loved. But if really seriously, why hadn't she been taken to hospital instead of being, as an earlier letter had described, looked after by the neighbour and the neighbour's daughter-in-law until Barbara turned up, five days after her first attack? Had it been inadvisable to move her? Or was it just that for spiritual reasons she 'couldn't' go to hospital? Bowen wished he knew more. He did at any rate know that many of Mrs Knowles's previous actions had been such as to make him object, but also such as to make him feel guilty for objecting. She was good at devising actions of that kind.

... relief not to have to go back to London yet especially this time of the year, I really think one more cocktail party would have killed me, they're all exactly the same and so are all the people we seem to meet, I can't bear their patter, they all talk exactly the same, they're all so incredibly catty and so dishonest, all trying to impress each other or do each other down the whole time. I do wish you didn't feel so tied to London the whole time, what a ghastly place it is, everyone leading unnatural lives and all of them perfectly miserable, you can feel it as soon as you arrive in the place, I can tell you I didn't lose any time getting from the air terminal over to King's Cross. You know Garnet we really ought to see if we can't get out of London sometimes for week-ends, of course a cottage would be lovely but they cost no end these days, still I'm sure there must be some nice little country pubs where we could put up quite cheap. I might be able to get a little bit of riding in then ...

Bowen could stand the idea of Barbara and her riding, since it was his faith that she did it out of a love of horses, not out of a love of being seen or known to frequent their backs, but he wished he could warn her of the appalling attendant dangers. You never knew the sort of people you

160

might meet in connexion with horses: auctioneers' wives, solicitors' daughters, dentists' mistresses, on a bad day even – he supposed dimly – aristocrats with titles, all talking horribly about horses and not about horses. And then there was this London thing, put in as if on purpose to bait him. Barbara had complained to him before that everyone there was the same, that she couldn't tell people apart (he found as little difficulty here as he found in telling female film-stars apart, another rare feat according to the kind of journalism she liked), but this was the first time he remembered her actually attacking the place, and cocktail parties in general as well, come to that. In his experience London was virtually staffed by people who said they didn't like London and cocktail parties by people who said they didn't like cocktail parties. He didn't say that. He liked London. He liked cocktail parties.

... *Mummy* ...

Aaoh! aoh! aooh! How had she managed to get back again? Eh? Perhaps the real reason for his attitude was that he was afraid there might be some truth in the old cow's conception of his character. Was he really, as she suggested by hints of a subtlety that Proust might have envied, a dipsomaniacal gourmand, a Dickensian work-housemaster in the home, a fang-bearing sadist towards his children, an aesthete when it came to doing a decent day's work and a navvy when he picked up a pen, a priapic fiend in marital relations? That last role was one which, during their visits to Mrs Knowles, he sometimes seemed to get near playing in Barbara's eyes. It was probably no more than that Mum had warned her off the old maggot so heartily in the past that even legal stuff appeared reprehensible with Mum just round the corner, getting up as she often did to pad past their room and switch off the landing light or the immersion heater, belting downstairs to let that

161

:sod of a dog in. Bowen had never decided whether she did this deliberately or at the prompting of some anti-erotic instinct. Whatever it was, last autumn a night of false starts, occasioned by some recurrent trouble with Mum's hot-water-bottle, had led him to take Barbara into some near-by woods the next afternoon for a little nature-ramble; a fine caper for a married man, he had said to himself rather bitterly, flicking a dead spider off the knee of his trousers.

... still it must have done you good to get away from things. I wish I were still with you. The kids are all being very good and send their love, David and Mark have some questions about God to ask you when you get back!!! Good boy about not playing Benny Himon's game about Strether. I'm sure you're doing the right thing. Look after yourself, podge, sometimes I want you so much I feel I could break in two. I love your ears. Love, love, love you.

yum yum yum yum yum

Barbie

x (bitey one)   X (open mouth one)

Bowen meditated for a moment on whether getting away from things had done him good, and then on the propriety of this concept. Then he thought about his wife's fondness for clauses on the pattern of 'I/you/we really ought to/ must see if I/you/we can't ...' They were the stylistic equivalent of her 'serious talk' face and posture. He wished he had the courage to inflict on her the pain of being told about the ways she got him down. But he hadn't and never would have. What made that certain were things like the closing phrases and interjections of her letter. No part of his nature could resist them or put reservations on what they stood for.

He looked idly through the other letters. Suddenly one of them took all his attention. He ripped it open.

Yes, it was from Baron Knowland all right. The text said that since Bowen was occupying furnished accommodation at the above address he had no security of tenure therefore agreement was at an end with effect from the last day of the month would he please find alternative accommodation as new tenants would be requiring to move in with effect from that date.

Bowen's mouth fell ajar. Unnoticed by himself, he belched. Yeah, Knowles and Knowland; that ought to have told him. The den. The table and chair and bit of carpet in the den. Furnished accommodation. New tenants. All the Bowen possessions out in the street. Five days to go till the end of the month. Barbara obviously can't do anything. Right, Benjamin Hyman, this is where you come in, boy. Cable – no, too late today; first thing in the morning.

Why did he mind this sort of thing so much? Perhaps it went to prove that he was an artist. He had thought in the past that his inability to follow any but the simplest abstract argument, his lack of zeal for washing-up and taking the current baby out in its pram, had suggested the very same thing. The case was starting to build up. Perhaps *Teach Him a Lesson* was a good idea after all.

15

Sitting drinking away under a tree in an important-looking thoroughfare called something like the Avenida da Liberdade, Bowen tried to feel full of fun. After all, here he was on the chair in the shade while everyone else was rushing about in the heavy morning sunshine. How did any work get done in this city? Perhaps none did. Secondly, he had access to as much drink as was good for him, or evensupportably bad for him : he had six of the large clean pieces of stage money left and any number of the small dirty ones. Thirdly, he had sent his cable; nothing more to be done except hope. Fourthly, old Buckmaster was off making 'a couple of business calls'. Fifthly, he was one day nearer to getting home than he had been yesterday. And a nice pole-axing lunch at one of Lisbon's best restaurants (which he had better pay for), a little doze in the car on the way back to Buckmaster's joint and an early retirement to bed would get him through most of today. And after that there were only four more full days until he sailed. If only he could somehow decide, just for his own satisfaction, whether Buckmaster was genuine or not. And if only, for that purpose, he could remember the significant thing he still fancied Emilia had said.

Buckmaster was now approaching with his long bounding stride, looking at everything with the delighted wonderment of a man just out of prison, or more likely a man just out of prison in a film. Bowen drank up his whisky-soda thing, of which he knew nothing except that it contained no whisky or soda and was bloody good.

'We'll go and see Fielding's tomb,' Buckmaster said, smiling.

'Will we? I thought we were going to have lunch.'

'Later. Lunch is late in these latitudes.'

'Shall we have a drink first?'

'Later, later. You would not, I take it, wish to visit Lisbon without spending a few minutes at Fielding's tomb?'

'Of course not.' Fielding himself would not be in attendance to chat to visitors, but it was a bit disrespectful of him not to seem keen to go and look at his tomb when asked, and he deserved sympathetic treatment for having been dead such a hell of a long time. And he had been a good

164

chap, too. Bowen realized he wanted to go very much. He could keep quiet about it when he got home.

'We could take a cab,' Buckmaster said, 'but it seems a pity that you should not extend as much as possible your regrettably small acquaintance with Lisbon. These strips of greenery are quite delightful, are they not? Such a refreshment to the senses, and with these magnificent palms ... Over there you will find a miniature cataract, all surrounded with ivy. This is the loveliest street I have ever seen, my friend.'

'Never been up Kingsway in Swansea you haven't, then, wus,' Bowen muttered to himself. But, although again he would have to be careful who he admitted it to, Lisbon was all right, and would be really worth while if it could somehow be got on rollers and shifted to about half-way between Brighton and Eastbourne. 'It must cost a lot of money to maintain,' he said to Buckmaster.

'Not so much, perhaps, as you might think, conditions being what they are . . . What have you to say of these beautiful pavements where we walk? Each of these tiny stones is shaped and fitted and levelled by hand – there could be no other way. Ah, there's much to be said for a land where machinery is costly and labour cheap and plentiful. Great wealth in the hands of a few, my dear Bowen, and petitioners at the gate, oh yes indeed.'

Wondering urgently whether he was doing the right thing, Bowen pulled him out of the path of a small fierce-looking yellow tram. This failed to quieten Buckmaster down in the least; indeed, he turned up the volume so that Bowen should miss as little as possible whenever a pedestrian or lorry might momentarily part them. The theme had now shifted from political theory back to the attractions of Lisbon. Bowen understood Buckmaster to say that getting to know a city was like getting to know a person: those that held themselves always a little aloof, that would not yield their secrets to the importunity of a mere acquaintance, that shrank back from a presumption of familiarity – these, and these alone, were they that no custom could ever stale, if he might be pardoned the phrase. Bowen thought not, on the whole, and hey, were cities really like that? Were people really like that, nice ones at any rate? Oh well, it had to be remembered that the old fellow either was or was pretending to be a great writer. Funny how those alternatives seemed to draw nearer and nearer together in his presence. He did look impressive, admittedly, loping along with his acutely white hat throwing half his prominent nose into shadow, his shoulders squared and his arms not swinging much. There was almost something of the prophet about him, the kind of prophet who got on rather better than elsewhere in places like Long Beach, Calif.

Bowen marvelled at the number of statues they passed: over the years, evidently, this part of the world had produced far more than its fair share of chaps who were pretty hot in their various lines. Not that the lines were all that various – the figures went in mainly for horse-riding, sword-brandishing, vestment-wearing and (a favourite pursuit) telescope-holding. Yes, the locals had been a tough little bunch in their day. The statues faded out and they went through some cobbled streets, empty except for old women in black who peered at them. Buckmaster suddenly rang a doorbell. A girl who was a nurse, or had dressed herself up to look like one, appeared. Buckmaster sounded as if he was asking after someone called Harry Grainger. Perhaps it was a password, for they were let in, then taken along a passage. Before Bowen could get properly started on wondering just what the hell was going on, they emerged into a church-yard, thickly planted with trees and tall shrubs. It was quiet and very lonely. In a few moments they were standing in front of a white stone sarcophagus raised on a platform. There was a good deal of Latin inscription. Everything was so clean and well looked after that it might have been put up the same year.

Buckmaster, just when he might have been expected to fly into a hortation, was silent. Bowen thought about Fielding. Perhaps it was worth dying in your forties if two hundred years later you were the only non-contemporary novelist who could be read with unaffected and whole-hearted interest, the only one who never had to be apologized for or excused on the grounds of changing taste. And how enviable to live in the world of his novels, where duty was plain, evil arose out of malevolence and a starving wayfarer could be invited indoors without hesitation and without fear. Did that make it a simplified world? Perhaps, but that hardly mattered beside the existence of a moral seriousness that could be made apparent without the aid of evangelical puffing and blowing.

Bowen was anxious to dissociate himself from the way Buckmaster was going on – hat in hand, head bowed, breath whistling through nostrils – but any remark might open the floodgates of English Men of Letters Series eloquence. In a moment the old boy replaced his hat and let his face relax into the stand-easy position. 'The darling of the comic muse,' he said efficiently.

'I admire him very much,' Bowen said.

'I too. I feel it an honour to stand in a company that is adorned by the presence of such a one.'

This was Buckmaster's way of saying, Bowen assumed, that he was as good as Fielding, or alternatively was putting on an act as one who thought so. In the circumstances no reply was possible. Bowen tried again to read some of the Latin on the tomb.

'But we are surely not to say,' it came rolling out, 'that the utterances of comedy, whatever their purity or power, can move us as we are moved by the authentic voice of tragedy. That alone can speak to us of the loneliness and the dignity of man. And this, my friend, means that much as I reverence this assured master of the picaresque I am unable to consider him my equal. In the field of the novel he is indeed the colossus of the eighteenth century, but I cannot feel that posterity will place him beside ... will care to place him beside the colossus of the twentieth.'

A monosyllable of demented laughter broke from Bowen before he had time to arrange a coughing fit. Too good to be true, eh? And so much too good to be true that Buckmaster must inevitably be able to see it like that as well. Bowen stopped coughing and his eyes went glassy. That was it. Of course. And immediately he remembered what it was Emilia had said that had struck him. He knew now what Buckmaster was. The evidence might not have convinced others, but it did him.

Buckmaster said awkwardly: 'These are not sentiments I would divulge except before such as you, my friend.'

'Naturally not.'

'Shall we go?'

They went. They had lunch. Bowen tried all he knew to pay for it, but Buckmaster wouldn't let him. Afterwards they went to the point where Buckmaster had arranged for the car to pick them up. It wasn't there. Buckmaster said violently: 'Mere selfishness. Inability to give attention to or even to comprehend the desires of others. One expects this, of course. Or one would expect it if one were not oneself blinded.'

His anger, visually signalled by a deep blush and jerky swallowings, was no real surprise to Bowen. From the moment they got into the car that morning it had been plain that Buckmaster and the chauffeur were having a little difference about something. Buckmaster had snapped at him; the chauffeur had moved his shoulders to and fro like a small girl enjoying a fit of temper. Buckmaster had been provocatively emphatic when they parted; the chauffeur had winked at Bowen, getting a cold stare in return, and had driven off as destructively as possible. In England such a scene, should it take place at all, must indicate something a bit special going on between Buckmaster and the chauffeur, but on this side of the water you could never be sure. Here passions and desires ran close to the surface, without regard for the empty ritualistic forms under which Anglo-Saxon provincialism had buried them, so that to find a grown man behaving like a child or an animal was nothing out of the way and could be related to any grade of emotion from peevishness upwards. You got used to it, presumably, if you lived over here long enough.

Buckmaster started churning out a long spiralling rigmarole of self-justification and apology. With notable self-restraint he inserted quite long episodes between the various statements of his recurrent theme about the difficulties of the artist. Exceptional men, he said, were likely to behave in exceptional ways, and said it as if he thought this was a justification for something or other, granted that it could be established as applying in any applicable case. Some of the rest of the time he talked about the ebb and flow to be discerned in all human relationships. Bowen could feel his eyes beginning to glaze over; he wanted the chance of mulling over his conclusions about the old boy, and of going to bed for twelve hours or so.

The car arrived, roaring, smoking, honking, pulling up with a squeal. A fairly long double bawling-out took place. A crowd collected, only a small one but comprehensive in that all age-groups and social strata seemed to be represented. It showed an interest that never approached partisanship and was individual rather than corporate, recalling the demeanour of English people watching a road-repair gang. Here and there was evident speculation as to why Bowen, although clearly involved in some way, was failing to join in. Otherwise he was left to himself. It occurred to him that it would be nice not to be there.

Having reduced the chauffeur to a shoulder-shrugging, scowling dummy, Buckmaster opened a rear door and motioned to Bowen. Under the influence of rage, the old life-enhancer looked all ears, nose and hat. They got in and were driven furiously away.

More apologies were offered and accepted. Buckmaster then fell asleep. So did Bowen. He had a dream about playing the xylophone to Oates and Afilhado which seemed very significant at the time. It lasted him most of the way back.

Feeling that his body had finally started to wear out in earnest, he went to his bedroom and wrote a short letter to Barbara. This, together with a completed article and other material, he took down to the post office and despatched. It took him a nice long time. He had another sleep and was woken by the sound of the gong, an instrument that had started life in Portuguese West Africa, or was it Portuguese East Africa? At dinner Buckmaster had little to say, seemingly still oppressed by the row with the chauffeur. Bowen tried to hint to him that at any rate he, Bowen, found nothing embarrassing or strange in the situation. He found Buckmaster much easier to talk to now that there was no longer any mystery about him. He wished he could tell him so.

About half-past ten they said good night. Bowen looked out of his bedroom window for some time. Beyond the level area round the house the land rose and fell in exaggerated undulations, like a relief model in geography. The soil was apparently too poor to support anything more ambitious than thin grass and a few trees that looked incapable of producing anything that people might want. Or perhaps it was just that Buckmaster had let the place run to seed. Why not? What a curious way to live. How could he manage without friends? And without neighbours? And without noise? At the moment it was almost totally quiet. The lorries passing on the road to or from Lisbon could be heard at this distance, but this was not much of a country for lorries. Not enough got produced which they could usefully carry about. At this time the characteristic sound was that of loud groaning creaks from the woodwork as the temperature went down. For the first couple of days these had startled him, but never as much as the pistol-shot noise produced when Oates creaked his way round the bungalow last thing and turned off the lights. He wondered how that representative of the Portuguese middle classes was getting on. Was he still having trouble from the awful people who, according to his own account, climbed over the wall at night and pulled up his plants because he was doing too well for himself with his job in Lisbon and his German motor-bike?

Bowen undressed and got into bed. It was a good bed and he soon felt too sleepy to think about Buckmaster. He thought about Barbara instead. He realized he had made up his mind that he was going to bring her abroad again next year however plain she might make it that she wanted to come. It was a pity he could never explain to her what a moving concession this was on his part. Perhaps he could work it so that Mrs Knowles opposed the plan. What a stroke that would be, whichever way it turned out. Anyway, an end to malice for the time being. Perhaps he could dream about Barbara if he put his mind to it.

Some time later he was dreaming that Bachixa had been made Pope when something woke him up with a jump. He listened. Then he heard a man calling out angrily in Portuguese – Buckmaster. It sounded just like the sort of thing he had bawled at the chauffeur that afternoon in Lisbon. There was silence for a time. Bowen began falling unquestioningly off to sleep again. There was a sudden loud bang of wood on wood from the end of the veranda where Buckmaster's room was: a door being flung open or a table or chair falling. A mixed-up disturbance followed, with two angry voices this time and things falling or being knocked into. It might have been a fight or it might have been a violent argument with people blundering about. Bowen sat up. He tried to tell himself that it was only like old Earl Knowland and his pal taking things to heart overhead in South Ken., but he was too afraid to believe himself. After another pause the disturbance started again, but without the voices. It seemed to move on to the veranda. He could hear someone panting. I am exactly the kind of man for this not to happen to, he thought.

Buckmaster's voice called: 'Bowen. Bowen.' Not loudly, but as if something physical was preventing him from calling loudly. Not loudly enough, perhaps, to wake Bowen up if he had been really sound asleep, but quite loudly enough to reach him in a waking state.

Bowen stayed absolutely still for a second. Then he jumped out of bed and ran out on to the veranda. Whatever it was was going on round the corner. Before he reached the corner there was a prolonged thumping noise. A second later he was there. A man standing near the top of the steps turned round when he heard him coming. He was dressed in a singlet and a pair of dark-coloured jeans, as the captain's father on *Suomi* had been, Bowen remembered. It was the chauffeur. As Bowen approached, the other bent into a sort of wrestler's crouch. Bowen kept moving. He had not hit anybody since the last line-out of the last match he had played in at St Helen's against the Scarlets (Swansea 11 pts., Llanelly 9 pts.) but now he got ready to do it again. They were still a few feet apart when the chauffeur laid his hand on the rail of the veranda and vaulted elegantly over it. Bowen heard him land – it was not a long drop – and run away round the side of the house.

The moon was bright enough for Buckmaster to be visible at once, lying on his back half-across the bottom step. He was moving about slightly. Bowen went down, stepped over him, then knelt. Something fearful seemed to have happened to Buckmaster's mouth. It was misshapen but Bowen could find no evidence of a blow. Then he had an idea and eased the lower jaw down. Yes, the old boy's false teeth were all over the place. Better take them out. He was doing this when Buckmaster's hand came up and made the adjustments. 'I can do it,' he said.

'How do you feel?'

'That treacherous devil. It's the last time I do anything for anyone.'

'Can you stand up?'

'Drew a knife on me. My leg hurts. They're all the same in the end. Nothing to choose between them.'

'Try and stand. Lean on me.'

'Sorry to be such an appalling nuisance. It's this leg.'

'Hold on here.'

When Buckmaster's left foot touched the ground he gasped and shuddered. Bowen helped him to sit down on the second step from the bottom with his leg out in front of him. They were both panting; Bowen realized he had been doing it almost ever since first coming out on the veranda. 'I'll get a doctor,' he said.

173

'I'm all right.'

'I can't move you without help and I'd be scared to anyway with that leg of yours. It feels normal to me but it might be broken; I wouldn't know. Does it hurt much now?'

'I can bear it.'

'Listen : where's your housekeeper?'

'The village. At her sister's. And she'd be no help if she were here. She's another of them.'

'How can I leave you, then? Supposing that chauffeur chap comes back?'

This seemed to bring Buckmaster round completely. 'Luis? What happened to him? Where is he?'

'He ran off before I got to him.'

'How typical. He will still be running, I have no doubt. Then some time tomorrow he will return, sobbing his repentance. I know the cycle, every stage of it.'

'Has he been as violent as this before?'

'Not quite. And so this time will be the last time.' Buckmaster gasped again and shivered. 'What a nuisance I am. Forgive me for involving you in this.'

Bowen went away and returned with a couple of blankets, some pillows, a bottle of whisky from the dining-room cupboard and a glass. He bestowed them appropriately about Buckmaster. Then he went away again and returned in jacket and trousers. 'Tell me where I can find a doctor,' he said.

'In the village, the white house on the right just past the café. He's an excellent fellow, young Madrigal. Most intelligent and reliable. Knowing that it is I who am afflicted he will come at once. He knows me as *o senhor inglês*, by the way. None of these people can pronounce my name.'

'I'll be back as soon as I possibly can. Is there anything else I can get you before I go?'

'Nothing, thank you.' Buckmaster smiled diffidently. He looked, with the blanket round his shoulders, like an old Red Indian, the wise one who keeps saying that the white man is his brother and there must be no more blood. 'How kind you are being to me, my friend, my dear Bowen. What a blessing to be in such good hands.'

In hands, anyway, Bowen thought to himself as he hurried off towards the road. He couldn't help feeling glad that so far he had been able to give all the things the situation had required of him, and such nasty things at the start, too. Then he felt less glad at the thought that not to have hesitated for that moment before rushing out of his bedroom might have saved Buckmaster from falling or being pushed down the steps, curse it. Might it? Would it? Probably it might and would, because he had always been that sort of chap. He badly wanted Barbara to suddenly manifest herself and tell him that of course it mightn't and wouldn't and he hadn't and wasn't. He hoped there was nothing still to come tonight which would find him wanting. There were plenty of things which would to choose from. He was that sort of chap too. Quite a number of his actions and attitudes had in the past struck him as unworthy of a man of his alleged sensibility, or a man of his age, or a man, but doing the necessary things about it was hard. Hard not because he didn't want to change, but because keeping on the alert for being mature and responsible and so on took it out of him. It was so seldom one got the amber light that would give one time to get everything nicely lined up for a spot of mature etc. behaviour. It would be quite okay if only he could manage to be a writer. Perhaps it wasn't too late even now. He remembered a woman with two Book Society Choices to her name telling him that the first qualification for being a writer was to be interested in yourself. Well, he ought to be well in, then.

He found Madrigal's house without difficulty and rang the bell hard and long. Get it over quickly. After a time a light went on upstairs, a head appeared at the window and a woman's voice asked him something.

'Senhor Madrigal?'

'*Nos da,*' she seemed to say.

'What? I mean *como?*'

'*Nos da, senhor.*'

He nearly broke down and cried at the thought of this fiendish conspiracy, the near-martyrdom at Buckmaster's designed only to lead up to him being bidden good night in the language of his native Wales.

'*Nos da, senhor,*' the woman repeated. '*Lisboa.*' He could see her pointing. '*Lisboa.*'

He got that all right. Why was everybody away tonight, then? Why hadn't he been prepared for this sort of thing? But he could hardly have been expected to copy down a little bilingual word-list at Buckmaster's dictation, could he? What the hell, then? '*Momento, senhora,*' he said. (Good stuff.) '*O senhor inglês.*' What was 'hurt'? Might be anything. What was 'ill'? '*Malade, malado, souffrant, souffrowng, souffranty.*'

'*Não compreendo.*'

Oh, Christ. What information about *o senhor inglês* would he be bringing to a doctor's house at this time? That the old boy wanted someone to scratch his behind for him? He went through a short ballet in the moonlight, wishing Emilia had got as far as 'leg' in her language-lesson. He pointed to his own leg. What about it? 'Not good'; that would do it. '*Não bom, não bom.*' He gave some yelps of simulated pain; this time he was reminded of Afilhado's '*owr, owr-owr*' routine. It all got a silent reception. '*Médico,*' he said desperately – he had got that off the doctor's sign on the *Rio Grande*: '*un autre ... um autro médico.*'

'*Outro médico, sim sim sim, compreendo.* Something or other *trese kilometros.*'

Thirteen bloody kilometres. That meant, what? sixty-five . . . eight miles as near as damn it, and shag it, and sod it. Eight miles one furlong, to be exact. Two hours at the very least. '*O carro?*' he asked, thinking that here at least was a sensible word.

There was more *nos da* and *Lisboa* stuff. Naturally. Madrigal would hardly have walked to Lisbon. No flies on Madrigal. Right. Setting his teeth, Bowen said : '*O carro du, do senhor inglês.*'

'*Sim?*' So what? her tone said.

'*O addresso do médico?* No good? Er ... *a casa do médico?* Where does he hang out, ducks?'

'*Compreendo.* Something *momento.*'

There was quite a long pause after the woman's head withdrew. It was a relief to have finished with dumb-crambo and word-making and word-taking for a bit. He heard the woman open a drawer. She must be getting dressed. She was going to take him there. All over bar the shouting. What would she be like? Pretty good if her voice was any guide. Mm. Were hornets active at night?

She wasn't going to take him there. Something pitched into the dust at his feet. It turned out to be a piece of paper wrapped round an empty scent-bottle. There was writing on the paper and what looked like a sketch map. Oh well, you couldn't blame her; she had put up with a lot and been very decent about it all. '*Obrigado,*' he called.

'*Bõa noite, senhor.*'

'*Bõa noite, senhora. Obrigado* very much.'

He went to Buckmaster and told him the score. The old fellow listened with an admirable effort at cheerfulness, but it was plain that his leg was giving him hell and he was getting cramped. 'If only I had had the telephone installed

177

here,' he said. 'But I was determined to keep myself isolated from the outside world. But wait: there's a kiosk in the village. I wish I had told you.'

'Never mind. Anyway, I can't be sure the chap'll come unless I go there and make him. Can you write me a note to give him?'

'Certainly. Are you used to continental roads?'

'Oh yes, I learnt to drive on them.' Drove a jeep into the back of a wireless truck belonging to 52 (Lowland) Division on them, in fact. 'Now don't you worry, I'll be back in less than half an hour, complete with doctor.'

Two minutes later Bowen was sitting feeling terrible in the driving seat. One by one he found his escape-routes closed: key in the ignition, petrol in the tank, all lights working. Well, he was used to the old left-hand drive, anyway. You had your right hand for the gears. And for the handbrake. Yeah, you could say that again.

The engine started first go off, the gear went in with hardly any dentist's-drill effect. 'Again the driver pulls on his gloves,' Bowen said, 'and in a blinding snow-storm, pity about that, starts upon his deadly journey, and again the writer runs howling to his art, well anyway.' The car began to creep nervously out of the little garage.

16

'Anyway, you made it.'

'Oh yes, I made it all right. I practically had to beat the doctor up to convince him I was serious. Then coming back I kept nearly knocking down chaps arrayed in traditional peasant costume, on their way to market, I suppose. It was still pitch dark, or moonlight, rather.'

'Colourful stuff.'

'Oh, colourful as a bastard. What about another of those?'

'No, let's go in.' When they were settled at their table, Bennie Hyman said: 'And how was old Buckmaster when you left him? Funny thing, I can't seem to get out of the habit of calling him that.'

'Neither can I. Oh, he was in pretty good shape, considering; quite perky and talking like mad. Apparently he hadn't broken his leg, or not properly. The doctor explained it all to me in Portuguese. He got a nurse in, the morning after it happened.'

'What was she like?'

'Wonderful. I've never seen so many gold teeth in one pair of human jaws in my life.'

'I suppose old Buckmaster . . . Christ, here we go again. I suppose Strether was all over you after that night.'

'You don't know the half of it, boy. Do you know, he wanted me to write a book about him? I soon crapped on that, as you can imagine. But I shall more or less have to get this article out; I can't see anything for it. That's going to be a hell of a chore.'

'A well-paid chore, though. You can sell it to the Yanks too.'

'You bet. Oh yes, the chauffeur turned up again, by the way, looking as if butter wouldn't melt in his mouth. Strether chucked him out of the house straight away. Made him cry.'

'Extraordinary business, all that.'

'I never did find out exactly what was going on. Didn't like to ask any of the questions I wanted to ask. I reckon the chauffeur was one of the boys all right, but that doesn't mean to say that Strether was up to any of the old nonsense. It could easily be a son-substitute thing.'

'You're very charitable all of a sudden. Ah, good morning, Fred.'

'Good morning, Mr Hyman. Good morning, sir.'

When they had ordered, Hyman said: 'Thank you for your cable, by the way – the second one, I mean. What put you on to things?'

'It was just something that happened when he and I were having a look at Fielding's tomb.'

'Cripes, you did have a cultural time, didn't you?'

'He said he thought he was better than Fielding, you see. He'd carried on in the same sort of way before, explaining he was part of the history of the English novel and all the rest of it, but this was really the pay-off. The way I looked at it, if he was a fake he'd have to be a pretty bright chap, about how people behave, I mean, and how people expect great writers to behave and so on. Because he'd fooled everybody up to then, myself included – I mean I'd been watching him at close range for days. Well then, given that sort of intelligence he wouldn't have dared to put himself on show as the kind of prancing, posturing phoney who'd say he was better than Fielding. Nothing to be gained by it. And far too much danger of affronting my conception of how great writers behave. He'd have been perfectly safe in sticking to humility, reverence and what-have-you. But he didn't. So that meant he couldn't have been putting on an act.'

'I think I follow you. But don't you in fact expect great writers to be prancing phoneys or whatever you said?'

'Of course I do, as far as people of the great-writer period are concerned, that is, that's between ... when exactly? Well, say roughly between *Roderick Hudson* and about 1930, death of Lawrence and the next bunch all just starting off – Greene, Waugh, Isherwood, Powell. Or perhaps 1939. But you couldn't expect Buckmaster to know I saw it like that. He'd grown up in that period himself, poor old devil. It couldn't possibly strike him in that way.'

'Was that the only thing that put you wise?'

'No, there was something else.' Bowen explained about Lopes and Emilia, omitting as irrelevant, and open to misinterpretation, the language lesson and its sequel. 'What I was trying to remember was that this girl had said 'Let us drink' or something *in English*. It was about the only thing she did say in English, perhaps it was the only thing she could say. But Buckmaster had never seen her before and all he knew was that she didn't speak *much* English. Which is a pretty wide concept. She might easily have been able to speak enough to tell me that from what she'd gathered he was a retired chamber-pot importer called Higginbotham. He wouldn't have dared let us out of his sight for a moment. Not if he'd been a fake. Far less risk to keep us there under his eye.'

'What about this blackmail stunt you thought this fellow Lopes might have been up to? He wouldn't have wanted you to see that, would he, old Buckmaster?'

'Oh, I soon came to the conclusion it couldn't be blackmail. His demeanour didn't seem right for that, especially not afterwards, and from what he said ... he didn't bother to concoct any sort of story. No, I think he was just afraid of a bit of a dust-up, a dispute over a debt, that kind of thing. He's the sort of chap who hates any, you know, unpleasantness. All through that chauffeur row I could tell he was loathing every minute of it.'

Hyman shook his head. 'Well, it all sounds rather finespun to me. I think you made up your mind you liked the old boy, even if he did bore you and put on this I'm-great-you-see act. And anyhow you were his guest. So you looked round for reasons for thinking he was what he claimed to be.'

'My mind doesn't work like that.'

'What? You're absolutely hopeless about people you like or who you think like you. People you don't happen to like never get a bloody chance and the others can get away with murder. They jump on your stomach and you lie there pointing out that their home circumstances were unfortunate.'

'Utter rubbish. Who jumps on my stomach?'

'Oh, well ... you know what I mean. All sorts of people, chaps you're friendly with and so on, some of those Welsh pals of yours particularly. You ... you give them too much rope. You let them kick you around too much.'

'Now you're talking like Barbara.'

'Well, she ought to know, oughtn't she? Still, we're getting away from the point. Let's finish off about the Buckmaster business. You got the right answer, that's the main thing, however you got it. Can I have another look at that photograph?'

Bowen took it out of its envelope and passed it across. It showed Buckmaster some twenty years younger, but unmistakably Buckmaster, sitting awkwardly at a café table opposite a man with a small mouth and an apostolic expression. Around them were various items of a continental nature. An inscription in ink mentioned John Wulfstan Strether and sincere friendship.

'We'll get that signature checked, of course,' Hyman said. 'But it's got to be genuine, hasn't it? Can't help being. Laurence Binyon. They shall not grow old, as we that are left grow old, but they're dead, aren't they? Can you beat it?'

'I had quite a time seeming honoured when he made me a present of that. He did so much want me to have it, it was extraordinary. And there was a lot of other stuff he said he hadn't had the heart to burn. Letters from Granville-

Barker urging him to write a play, that kind of caper. I reckon there must have been about half a dozen chaps who knew who he was, but he made sure they were the kind to keep their mouths shut. Well, Bennie, what about it? Do I get that job or not?'

Hyman sighed. 'Afraid not, chumbo,' he said, blushing slightly. 'Old Weinstein was delighted with your bit of special investigation. But he's promised a frightful little turd of a failed barrister that he can come in in the autumn. So that's that. I really am sorry. I'm going to get Weinstein to write you a personal letter explaining the whole thing. Then perhaps you won't think I was leading you up the bloody garden about it all.'

'That's all right, Bennie, don't you worry.'

'I feel very mean about it.'

'Well, don't. You did your stuff for me over that land-lord business. I saw him last night when I got in. He'd brushed his hair specially and his voice was about half the volume it usually is. He kept on hoping I'd find everything satisfactory, felt awfully cut up about the unfortunate mis-understanding there'd been, it had got him down no end. What did you do to him?'

'Oh, we got by on abuse and threats, really. Your cable didn't give us a great deal to go on, you see. Not that it mattered. He started apologizing as soon as he laid eyes on old Levine. Couldn't blame him.'

'You know, he put in a lot of work persuading me to go on using the room we had the dispute about in the first place. It was important to his well-being that I should.'

'Let me know any time he needs a refresher course.'

'I'll do that.'

'Mind you do. You're not looking too bright, Garnet. Bit on the shagged side.'

'Yes, I need a holiday.'

'Was it a complete wash-out in Portugal?'

'Oh no, I wouldn't say that. Some of the time it was hardly any worse than it is here. That's when you start thinking you really love it and must come back the first chance you get. I've been thinking it over. I think what it is, there's such a host of things that can go wrong, so many more than there are here, that when you're not actually being eaten up by insects and your guts aren't playing hell with you and an official isn't telling you your papers aren't in order and nobody's putting you right in the picture about the local writers and you've got a decent bed and you aren't writhing about with sunburn and there aren't any smells to speak of and you haven't got to start looking for a hotel and in general you won't have to deal with anybody for the rest of the day and you've got something to read, well then you tell yourself you're having a bloody marvellous time. You know, like it was in the war. Remember how tremendous it was in the canteen having sausages and chips and a cup of tea and listening to the Forces' Programme? While some poor sod in the same barrack-room was on guard? Same idea. Going abroad teaches you how important small comforts are. But I knew all about that already, see? And then there's the weather. It does make everything seem romantic, there's no getting away from that. But aren't we supposed to have grown out of all that type of stuff? It's just as much an evasion as looking at the telly, only more expensive and you can't stop it when you want to and go out to the pub, you have to wait for your ship. Then when you get home you realize how much you like it here. If that wasn't another thing you knew already, that is.'

'The old closed mind, eh? It's a nice mind, but it does sound a bit on the closed side, you must admit.'

'Closed against what? I'm ready for things to happen to me all right, as long as they aren't too nasty. I can't stop them, anyway. But they have got to happen and they have got to happen to me. And by the way I don't object to doing a few things too, just now and then, as well as having them happen to me. But going abroad isn't going to actually help on any of that. Going and standing on the touchlines of other chaps' ways of life and telling yourself you're joining in isn't very self-aware. Just like going through foreign poetry with the dictionary and telling yourself you're reading it. If you put in ten years learning the language you can start to be some use at it. But how many people can afford to go into it all properly?'

'I seem to remember you telling me about one or two things that happened to you in Portugal.'

'Yes, but they weren't specifically abroad things. It would have been quite easy to duplicate my little expedition in search of the doctor in several areas in North Wales, for instance. I know they dress differently there, but people hurt their legs and have to get chaps to help them in much the same way. Still, I shouldn't like you to get the idea I'm trying to knock Portugal and the Portuguese. It's a very nice-looking place all round and if you exclude the Government and the upper classes the people are as decent as you'd find anywhere. It's just that the place is located abroad and the people are foreigners, which for the purposes of this discussion merely means that they and I belong to different nations, so we can't understand each other or get to know each other as well as chaps from the same nation can. I'm all for international co-operation and friendship and the rest of it, but let's be clear what we mean by it. My God, is that the time? Can you hurry that chap, do you think?'

'Sure, if you'll talk less. How long have you got?'

'I'll have to be out of here by a quarter to to do it comfortably. So that I can get a bus, I mean.'

'How long have they all been up there?'

'Long enough, really. They were due back the day before yesterday, you see, but something seems to have prevented them from doing that, somehow. Something to do with mother-in-law not wanting them to go or something. Something like that, anyway.'

As they were leaving the restaurant Bowen caught sight of the rear elevation of a female book-critic he knew. It was just doubling itself up to get into a taxi. The need to trot forward and kick it came upon him. There could be no doubt but that the woman was on her way to finish an article commending, or possibly questioning, someone's ability to convey the veritable tang of Galicia. Still, she had probably lived there for a few months, and if so an austere, stern pity should be lavished upon her. He permitted her to withdraw without molestation. After all, she had to use up her stuff somehow. He vowed to himself never to divulge his knowledge that Salazar and Franco had had to get together to stop the Portugal-Spain soccer matches with their attendant knife-fights, that in Silves the first Christian king of Portugal and Richard Lion-Heart had got together to massacre 30,000 Moors whom they had promised safe conduct.

'I'm sorry about that job,' Hyman said. 'Really.'

'Give it a rest. What about getting drunk one evening?'

'You'd better watch yourself, you know. Got to keep in trim for when you have to squire Strether round London.'

'I'll trim your . . . I'll ring you up.'

'Fine. Remember me to the family.'

They took their leave. Bowen got on his bus. He let himself think for a moment about *Teach Him a Lesson*, which he had read carefully through on the boat and then torn

186

up. It had been bad in the kind of way that he had formerly thought only great writers capable of. But he was going to write something else instead, about a man who was forced by circumstances to do the very thing he most disliked the thought of doing and found out afterwards that he was exactly the same man as he was before. Nobody, nobody at all, was going to hear anything about it until it was finished.

He gazed out of the window. London was looking full of good stuff. Admittedly it, together with most of the rest of the United Kingdom, was the land of Sorry-sir (sorry sir bar's closed sir, sorry sir no change sir, sorry sir too late for lunch sir, sorry sir residents only sir), but one couldn't expect to win all the time. He found after a moment that he was thinking of Emilia and the wonderful foreign look she had had that nobody had ever told her about. He realized he had not been quite straight with Bennie Hyman, or with himself, about why he had come to the conclusion that Lopes couldn't be blackmailing Strether. It was simply because he had decided that Emilia couldn't be a blackmailer's girl. And he had decided that because he had liked Emilia. But of course in spite of that she could be a blackmailer's girl. So perhaps it was true that he let people he liked get away with murder. But what did that matter? What did matter was that Emilia almost certainly was a blackmailer's girl. How sad and horrible that was.

The girl he was going to meet, at any rate, could never conceivably be a blackmailer's girl. That was a big point about her. In fact it was emblematic of the biggest point of all about her, the biggest point there could be about anybody.

A few minutes later the non-blackmailer's girl was hurrying down the platform to meet him. She left Sandra to totter along between the two boys, put her suitcases down and bounded up to him like a little agile tennis-player. They kissed. Bowen had never felt so relieved in his life.

'Oh, bogey,' Barbara said. 'You look a bit tired.'

'I'm fine.'

'But you're lovely and brown. I think your holiday's done you a lot of good.'

FOR THE BEST IN PAPERBACKS, LOOK FOR THE 🐧

In every corner of the world, on every subject under the sun, Penguin represents quality and variety – the very best in publishing today.

For complete information about books available from Penguin – including Pelicans, Puffins, Peregrines and Penguin Classics – and how to order them, write to us at the appropriate address below. Please note that for copyright reasons the selection of books varies from country to country.

BY THE SAME AUTHOR

Titles published or in preparation

The Alteration
The Anti-Death League
The Egyptologists
Ending Up
Girl, 20
The Green Man
I Want It Now
Jake's Thing
Lucky Jim
The Old Devils
One Fat Englishman
Riverside Villas Murder
Russian Hide-and-Seek
Stanley and the Women
Take a Girl Like You
That Uncertain Feeling